CHIEF EXECUTIVE

NICOLETTE DANE

CONTENTS

ABOUT THE AUTHOR

Nicolette Dane landed in Chicago after studying writing in New York City. Flitting in and out of various jobs without finding her place, Nico decided to choose herself and commit to writing full-time. Her stories are contemporary scenarios of blossoming lesbian romance and voyeuristic tales meant to give you a peep show into the lives of sensual and complicated women. If you're a fan of uplifting and steamy lesbian passion, you've found your new favorite author.

www.nicolettedane.com

SIGN UP FOR NICO'S MAILING LIST!

If you'd like to be notified of all new releases from Nicolette Dane and receive a FREE story, point your web browser to https://readni.co and sign up for Nico's mailing list right now!

ONE

*W*ith her hands together on her desk, Nadia Marek stared blankly at the open door to her office. It was Monday morning, and the meeting with her company's new CEO would soon begin. Everything was happening so fast, and it was making Nadia's head spin. But she knew this buy-out was ultimately a good thing. It was the move that could take Color Wheel, the advertising agency she worked for, to the next level.

Nadia had begun her time at Color Wheel as a graphic designer. But her skills and dedication brought her to the next stage of her career, account manager for one of the company's largest clients. Polly was a huge smartphone brand, known all over the world, and Color Wheel was in charge of their North American marketing and advertisement. And Nadia was in charge of that. What had begun as just a small, boutique firm in Chicago had grown to something massive.

Which is how they drew the attention of Scheffler & Vonn, the storied and venerated agency that handled many of the largest brands in the country. It was Scheffler & Vonn that had bought out Color Wheel, and it was today that they were installing a new CEO.

"Nadia," said a smiling woman who was now standing at the door. She gave the door a few light knocks to try to wake Nadia from her reverie. "You there, babe?"

"Huh?" said Nadia. She blinked a few times and then saw Laurie standing there waiting, still smiling. Laurie was an account manager like Nadia, and they had come up in the company together. They were both in their mid-thirties, both brunettes, and had been friends now for a number of years. "Oh, hey there."

Laurie stepped into Nadia's office and delicately sat down in a chair in front of the desk.

"It's going to be okay," said Laurie. "They're not going to change much, if anything. Frances told me so."

"Frances is only going to stick around for as long as they made her in the buy-out agreement," said Nadia. "Then she's going to take all her money and go live on an island." Laurie laughed.

"I don't know," she said. "Frances is pretty type-A. I bet she'll just start another business."

"If I just sold a company for twenty million dollars, I think I'd give myself a little bit of rest," said Nadia.

"Well, you're not Frances," countered Laurie.

"Well, yeah," Nadia replied. "And anyway, how are things *not* going to change? This is Scheffler & Vonn we're

2

talking about. They have a way of doing things. They've been in business like seventy years. I can just picture them storming in here, holding tumblers of whiskey, smoking cigars, and asking me to pick up their dry cleaning."

"So you're worried that the historically very male dominated institution of Scheffler & Vonn is going to come into our very female agency and tell us to get back into the kitchen?" Laurie asked, lifting a brow. "Is that what's bugging you?"

"I mean, when you put it that way," said Nadia. "No, I don't *really* think that. But I do worry that we might be treated as though we're not all that serious or important."

"Are you worried that they're going to come in here and just pluck our big clients away?" said Laurie. "Because that thought *has* actually crossed my mind."

"I've worked so hard on Polly," said Nadia. "I would just be angry as hell if they took them away from me and gave them to one of their own teams. I can't even entertain that thought right now or I'll just be fuming."

"Frances assured me that we didn't have anything to worry about," said Laurie. "Keeping things more or less how they are, at least for the time being, was part of the deal."

"Things can change," said Nadia. "This is a competitive business. And you know they only bought us so that they no longer needed to compete with us."

"We're going to be okay," Laurie said with a refreshed smile. "Let's not worry about things that haven't yet come to pass."

"You're right," Nadia acquiesced. "It might be just fine. We'll get a new Frances, and maybe she'll be just like the old Frances."

"Maybe better," Laurie said, trying to remain positive. "Maybe she won't call you just as you're laying down for the night to ask about some mundane detail that could have waited until morning." Nadia laughed softly.

"She's a bit crazy," mused Nadia. "But she's been a good boss. I'll miss her."

"She's not gone yet," said Laurie.

"But probably soon," said Nadia.

"Probably soon," repeated Laurie.

Nadia picked up her phone and checked the time. She sighed and then looked back to Laurie.

"I think the meeting will be starting shortly," said Nadia.

"You want to head over there?" asked Laurie.

"Yeah," said Nadia, standing up and grabbing a note-book. "I guess it's time."

Laurie smiled and stood up as well. The two women exited Nadia's office and made their way down the hall.

As they entered the meeting room, other members of staff from Color Wheel were filing in as well. The account managers were there, team leads for the various departments, a few people from HR, and the head of the administration department. Already standing at the front of the large table were Frances, a woman in her late fifties with big glasses and her peppered gray hair back in a tight bun, and another woman who Nadia didn't recognize.

4

This woman, however, was absolutely stunning. Nadia almost couldn't take her eyes off of her.

The woman had an athletic build, slim yet firm, and she stood with her shoulders back and arms crossed. She wore a black suit with a white button-down underneath it, unbuttoned into a plunging neckline with a wide collar. Her hair was blonde and chin-length, though it had a curl to it and it was immaculately styled. This woman looked powerful and she looked rich.

"Who is that?" Nadia whispered to Laurie as they took their seats.

"I don't know," said Laurie. "I'm guessing our new boss."

"I think we're all here," announced Frances, looking around the room as everyone found a seat at the table. She adjusted her glasses and scrunched her nose. "This looks like everyone."

The woman standing next to her smiled and gave Frances a single nod, as though she were signaling her agreement.

"Okay, Color Wheel," said Frances, addressing the group. "Thank you all for being here this morning. I know Monday mornings can be a little hectic, so I appreciate that we were all able to make time to attend. As you all know, Color Wheel has been bought by Scheffler & Vonn. It's a deal that has been in the works for a while, and it has finally gone through. And it's a big deal for us. It's going to allow Color Wheel to really hit the next level and give our clients even better service."

There was some light applause from the group. Nadia joined in after a moment.

"Yes, thank you," said Frances, waving the applause off. "Now, I know you're all wondering if things are going to change around here and the answer to that is *mostly no*. Scheffler & Vonn aren't looking to change a good thing, and Color Wheel is definitely a good thing right now. But some smaller things might change, to those specific changes I can't really speak. What I can speak to, however, is my own position. I'll be here for the next couple months to help the transition, after which I will no longer be needed."

The group lightly chattered, causing the overall feeling to be one of concern.

"It's not a big deal," Frances reassured them, holding a palm up. "This is part of the agreement and it's what I wanted. During the transition, I'll be passing on my knowledge of the company to others and leading us all will be our new CEO. Color Wheel, let me present to you, from Scheffler & Vonn, Miss Avery Wool."

As Frances motioned to the woman standing next to her, the group applauded. Avery smiled and bowed her head. Nadia focused in on her, looking her up and down. She was beautiful and Nadia couldn't help but feel enamored with her new boss. Avery was one of the most attractive women that Nadia had ever seen.

"Thank you, Frances," said Avery, in a firm and serious voice. "I sincerely appreciate the warm welcome."

Frances smiled and then she took a seat herself.

"As Frances said," Avery began. "My name is Avery

Wool and I am formally the chief administrative officer of Scheffler & Vonn. I grew up in Connecticut and have lived and worked for the last twenty years in New York City. I attended Harvard Business School and got my start in real estate, with my family's company M. M. Wool Properties, which owns and operates many buildings in New York. I joined Scheffler & Vonn six years ago and have worked as an executive ever since. And now I have moved here to Chicago to take over as your CEO and to assist in making Color Wheel an even greater firm than it already is."

The group applauded and Avery smiled knowingly.

"We intend to change nothing," Avery said once the applause ended. "Scheffler & Vonn acquired Color Wheel because of your impressive client base, as well as your talent in the industry. We had grown tired of trying to compete with you, so joining forces seemed like the next best option. I want you to maintain business as usual during this transition, keep our clients happy, and simply do your jobs to the best of your ability."

There was chatter among the group, nods in agreement, and a general acceptance of Avery's words. Nadia still felt uneasy about the transition, mostly worried that Polly would be taken from her, but at the same time she had a difficult time taking her eyes off of Avery. She could command a room, and she exuded power and control. With mixed feelings on her mind, Nadia looked over at Laurie for a moment. Laurie just smiled.

"Any change we do make," Avery went on. "Will be superficial. Your pay stubs will come from a different payroll processing company, and the day of the week you get paid on will change. You're biweekly right now?" she asked Frances.

"That's correct," Frances answered.

"Our payroll will be semi-monthly," Avery announced. "It's not a big change, it's just how we do things and we'll need to keep it uniform. PTO is handled a little differently, you'll be put on our health plan. It's all just minor administrative changes. But as for how you work with your clients and the artistic side of things, we're going to leave you to do what you do best. In the meantime, I'll be scheduling meetings with many of you to get a handle on your positions and how you function here at Color Wheel. About a month from now, we'll have another all-hands meeting and we'll start planning for the future."

Avery smiled and looked down to Frances, waving her hand softly as if to ask if Frances had anything to add. Frances just smiled in return and shook her head.

"It's so great to meet you all," Avery said. "Now let's get back to work."

The group applauded for a final time and people began standing up. Nadia and Laurie stood up together, though Nadia's eyes were concentrated on Avery, who was now speaking softly with Frances.

"See, that wasn't so bad," said Laurie. "She seems perfectly fine. There's no need to worry."

"Yeah," agreed Nadia with some skepticism. "It wasn't bad. Is it just me, or is Avery *really* hot?"

"Nadia!" said Laurie, laughing at Nadia's revelation. She

looked up toward the head of the table and considered Avery for a moment. "Yeah, I guess she is pretty hot."

"She's stunning," said Nadia, shaking her head.

"Let's go get a coffee," Laurie said, smiling as she placed her hand on Nadia's shoulder.

"Okay," Nadia agreed.

Nadia took one more peek up at Avery, and as she did this Avery locked eyes with her. Nadia suddenly felt frightened, she looked away, and she hurriedly followed Laurie out of the meeting room with all the others.

Avery watched as Nadia left, and she smiled coyly to herself.

Sitting on the couch in her condo living room, sipping from a glass of wine, Nadia looked down longingly into her phone screen. On it was a picture of her ex-girlfriend, Lucy. It had been about six months since she and Lucy had broken up, and Nadia still wasn't completely over it. Lucy had gotten the opportunity to join a tech start-up in San Francisco, and she wanted Nadia to go with her. Nadia, however, had just landed the Polly account and was working over-time, dedicating herself to her career at Color Wheel.

Neither woman would budge. They both had their careers to think of and just like that it was over. Nadia took another drink, she sighed, and she remembered Lucy fondly.

Ever since being promoted from graphic design to

account management, Nadia's job had grown hectic. Her breakup with Lucy was a portent for her life after the promotion. There was little time for a relationship with the amount of work she had on her plate. But her career was important to her. It was the most important thing in her life.

And Lucy probably knew that.

Nadia's condo was in a completely rehabbed industrial building in the West Loop. The walls were brick, the ceilings were high, the windows were large. It had an open layout, with a partition wall to block off her bedroom that she'd had built after buying the place. Tastefully decorated and modern, the loft condo was Nadia's respite from her frenetic work world.

An echoing knock came from Nadia's door. Setting her glass and her phone down on the coffee table in front of her, Nadia leapt up and scurried across the room. When she approached the door, she quickly looked through the peephole and then yanked the door open.

"Hey," she said blithely. Standing outside the door was Laurie. Not only did the women work together, but Nadia had also hooked her friend up with a condo in the building a few years back.

"Hi," said Laurie. She was dressed down for the evening, wearing short cotton sleeping shorts, a tank, and flip-flops. In her hand was a bottle of wine. "Care for a drink?"

"I'm way ahead of you," Nadia replied with a laugh. She stepped out of the way and Laurie waltzed in.

As Nadia moved back toward the couch, Laurie went to the kitchen area, opened her bottle of wine, grabbed a glass from the cupboard, and then sashayed over toward her friend. She plopped down on the couch, poured herself a glass of wine, and then refilled Nadia's glass.

"I've got this idea for a viral video for Polly," Nadia said, leaning over and picking up her notebook from the table. "There will be this pirate and his parrot and—"

"We don't need to talk about work," said Laurie, interrupting her. "It's after eight. We're drinking wine. I'm in my PJs. Polly can wait until tomorrow."

"Yeah?" said Nadia, her face softening, like she was glad that Laurie had let her off the hook. "You're right." She tossed her notebook back down.

"Leave it at the office, you know?" said Laurie. "I know you can't control when ideas come to you, and I know you feel a lot of pressure, but you'll perform much better if you give yourself a break and just chill."

"I know," said Nadia. "I guess I'm just trying to occupy myself. I've really been in my head lately."

"With the buy-out?" asked Laurie. "The new boss?"

"Yeah, all that," said Nadia. "And I've just been thinking about Lucy lately. I sometimes wonder if I made the right decision."

"Lucy was sweet but you two had different visions," said Laurie, taking a drink from her glass. "She had to get out to San Francisco if she really wanted to thrive in her work, and that wasn't what you wanted to do. You have a great thing going right here."

"Maybe I'm just lonely," said Nadia. "I guess it just feels crummy to be 35 and alone again."

"Hey, I'm 35 and alone," joked Laurie. "You don't see me crying about it."

"Yeah, but that's because you're like Mary Tyler Moore or something," said Nadia. "You're the quintessential professional woman who thrives on it."

"Sure, but that doesn't mean I don't want a relationship," said Laurie. "But the right guy is going to have to fit into my life as I like it. I think that's the same for you. Lucy wasn't the right girl for you in that regard."

"I know, but she was so cool," Nadia said in a mock-whine. "She was like a cool hipster geek. She had tattoos. And she was a brilliant computer programmer."

"Lucy was cool," said Laurie. "I agree. But maybe she was a little too freewheeling for you. She moved across the country with nothing but a backpack. You're a little more conservative than that."

"I guess I prefer more stability," confirmed Nadia.

"You do," said Laurie. "Hey, I'm the same way. But just because I haven't found my perfect guy yet, that doesn't mean I'll never find him. We're all on our own journey."

"Your last guy," said Nadia. "Ben, right?"

"Right."

"What was wrong with him?" Nadia asked.

"We had fundamentally different views about a really important topic," said Laurie, already refilling her wine. "He wanted kids, I don't."

"Oh yeah," said Nadia. "I remember."

"And a few arguments ensued because of it," Laurie went on. "But it was an incompatibility we just couldn't get past. There would have been too much resentment had either one of us given in."

"I don't want kids either," said Nadia. She leaned over, wrapped both of her arms around Laurie's arm, and rested her head on Laurie's shoulder. "Maybe you could be my girlfriend." Laurie laughed.

"You would hate dating me," said Laurie. "I'm selfish in bed, my bathroom is a mess, and I drink too much wine." She took a big gulp from her glass.

"I could get over all of that," Nadia said, keeping up the ruse.

"Plus," said Laurie. "I don't like to eat pussy."

"Damn it!"said Nadia, pushing herself off of Laurie and throwing her arms in the air. "I just can't win." Laurie laughed again.

"If I did," said Laurie. "You know I'd definitely give yours a try, sweetie."

"I know," said Nadia, smiling deeply at her friend.

"There's a fine lady out there for you," Laurie went on. "I just know there is. You're an amazing person, you're kind, you're hardworking, you're honest. You're an absolute catch, Nadia, and I don't think you have anything to worry about."

"Thank you," Nadia said in earnest. "That means a lot."

"Is there anybody you're interested in?" asked Laurie. "Anybody at all?"

"I don't know," said Nadia. "You know, Avery Wool is pretty gorgeous but how crazy would I have to be to try to chat *her* up?" Nadia laughed and Laurie joined her.

"Yeah, that would be something," said Laurie. "But you're not seriously interested in Avery, are you?"

"I don't even know her," Nadia said. "I don't know anything about her."

"I don't think she's married," said Laurie, smiling impishly. "Maybe she's who I'll become in the future. Super hot, forty-something lady, CEO of a company, looking like I've really got my act together. She's a little intense, but I think she's earned it."

"Yeah, I mean, I respect the hell out of her," said Nadia. "That, and her good looks, if there's anybody in my life that I have a crush on, it's probably her."

"Well, keep dreaming," said Laurie, rubbing Nadia's shoulder blade tenderly. "Maybe your dreams will come true."

"Maybe," said Nadia. She took another long drink from her wine glass and then put on a fatigued smile aimed at her friend. The thoughts of Avery that danced in Nadia's head were easily dismissed as fantasy. Instead, she wondered if she'd ever find a partner. She wondered if she'd put too much focus on work, and not enough on love.

"Oh, sweetie," said Laurie, easily able to read Nadia's feelings in her face. "Come back over here." Laurie guided her friend to her side, letting Nadia once again hug her arm and rest her head on Laurie's shoulder. Laurie delicately petted Nadia's hair.

"I'm okay," said Nadia. "Really."

"Do you want to talk about something else?" asked Laurie. "Anything?"

"Can we talk about work?" said Nadia. "About my idea?"

"Sure," Laurie said with a reassuring smile. "Tell me your idea. I'm all ears."

NADIA SAT ALONE in one of the small conference rooms in the office, in a cushy leather chair behind an oak table. The room was windowless, with a bookshelf against one wall and a television mounted to the wall opposite. Her fingers knitted together as she waited. In front of her was her notebook, next to it her closed laptop and a brown file folder.

Her nerves were getting to her. She just wanted to get this meeting over with. Laurie had already had her meeting and it went fine, but there was still something in the back of Nadia's mind telling her that it was going to be a disappointment. Things were going to change, and not for the better. This buy-out had really thrown her career plans for a loop.

Just when Nadia felt she could no longer handle her own impatience, the conference room door swung open and Avery walked in. She closed the door behind her and then approached the table with a smile.

"Good morning," said Avery. "You must be Nadia Marek."

"Yes," said Nadia, quickly standing up. She reached her hand across the table. "Pleased to meet you."

"And you, as well," said Avery, accepting Nadia's hand and shaking it. She had a firm grip. "Let's have a seat."

Nadia nodded, and retook her seat. Avery pulled out the chair across the table from her and sat down.

"Nadia," mused Avery, pulling a folder out of her attache and opening it up on the table in front of her. She looked over some of the included paperwork. "You've been with the company for seven years?" she asked without looking up.

"That's correct," said Nadia.

"You began your tenure here as a graphic designer?" Avery said, looking at Nadia now and smiling.

"Yes," said Nadia. "That's my background, but recently I was promoted to manage the account of one of our biggest clients. Polly."

"I see that," said Avery, offering a slow nod in agreement.

"I also do some creative direction," Nadia continued. "I wear a few hats, really. We're not organized so typically as a company like Scheffler & Vonn might be."

"Polly is indeed quite a big client," said Avery. "How did you manage to get that responsibility?"

"I did a lot of design work for them," said Nadia. "I was doing their print ads, billboards, and I even did some story-boarding for their commercials. I developed a rapport with their marketing manager, this gentleman named Harold Rauk, and Frances thought that I would do a good job managing the account." Nadia paused and gave a short, nervous laugh. "This kind of feels like I'm interviewing for my job."

"Maybe you are," Avery said with an impish grin.

Nadia's eyes widened and surprise hit her. "Relax," Avery said after a moment. "I'm just getting to know you. You're not interviewing for your job."

"That's a relief," said Nadia, smiling for the first time. She took a deep breath and relaxed into her chair. "I haven't really known what to expect about this meeting."

"This meeting is so that I can get a handle on how Color Wheel operates on a day-to-day basis," said Avery. "Once I better understand operations here, I can make any adjustments that might be needed for the company to function more efficiently. Scheffler & Vonn has many systems at its disposal, many of which Color Wheel might be able to take advantage of and use to better thrive in an increasingly competitive environment."

"Wow, okay," said Nadia, smiling and nodding. "I think that sounds good. You know, I'm pretty serious about my position here. I honestly love this career and I work very hard at it. Getting Polly's account was a huge score for me, and a responsibility I take seriously as I think many people around here could attest. I think we've got a good thing going and while I'm not eager for too much change, I like the idea of utilizing Scheffler & Vonn to up our game."

"That's great to hear," said Avery. "You know, Nadia," she said, pausing for a moment to consider her words. "I've taken particular interest in you because of the Polly account. It really is a big deal. They're a major smartphone manufacturer and a leader in the technology."

"Oh yeah," Nadia agreed. "They're huge."

"And it was after Color Wheel got the Polly account that

Scheffler & Vonn began to take notice," Avery continued. "You do know that we lost the bid to you guys."

"I do know that," admitted Nadia sheepishly.

"We decided, ultimately, that it would be cheaper in the long-term to just buy you out rather than to continue losing clients to you," said Avery. She stopped and chuckled softly to herself. "Scheffler & Vonn is very old school, and I think the wrinkles are beginning to show."

"Well, they can't be *too* old school if they hired a female executive," said Nadia, smiling in fellowship.

"They pick their battles," Avery said evenly. "I'm not sure many would call it a promotion to go from a C-level position at Scheffler & Vonn to token CEO at one of their new acquisitions. But for me, it's the title and the possibility that—" She stopped herself and just blithely smiled, as though she were papering over any kind of truth that might come out. "I am happy for the opportunity to pilot such a female-centric ship as Color Wheel."

"I didn't mean anything by my comment," said Nadia. "I was just trying to compliment the company."

"I understand," said Avery. "Marek," she said, changing the subject. "What's the origin of that name?"

"It's Polish," said Nadia. "Polish and Czech. My grand-parents immigrated from Poland after the war."

"Ah yes," said Avery. "I can see that now."

"What about your name?" Nadia asked. "What's Wool?"

"At one point in my family history," said Avery. "It was Woolen. It's an English surname. But my great-great-grandfather shortened it to Wool before he started our family real estate business."

"It's pretty cool that you know your family history back so far," said Nadia. "And that your company has been around for such a long time."

"It is," Avery said with a smile. "Nadia, I think you have control of the Polly account and I'd like to see you flourish with it. I would like to work a little closer with you and with the account, if you don't mind."

"If I don't mind?" repeated Nadia. "Yeah, sure. Of course. You are the boss, after all." Avery laughed.

"That is true," she said. "I was being polite in asking your permission to do what I intended on doing anyway." Now Nadia laughed.

"I appreciate the honesty," said Nadia. "I prefer honest, even if it's bad news. Reading between the lines isn't always fun for me. It's too much like a game."

"But games can be fun," countered Avery. "Games keep you guessing. They make things more exhilarating. I think anticipation is wonderful. It gets me excited." As she said this, Nadia noted the excitement growing in Avery's face.

"Sure," said Nadia, simply agreeing with her boss so as not to step on her toes. "I can understand that feeling."

"Thank you for making the time to come and see me," said Avery. She pushed back from the table and stood up. Nadia, feeling surprised by the abruptness, mimicked Avery's move and stood up as well.

"That's it?" said Nadia.

"That's it," replied Avery. "Let's meet again soon to go

over the specifics of Polly's account. A little less formal. I'll stop by your office in the next couple of days."

"Of course," said Nadia. "I can make time whenever for you."

"I wouldn't want to pull you from any client work," said Avery. "So if you're deep in the middle of something, feel free to be honest about that and not bend to me because of who I am. No games, after all. Right?" She grinned.

"Right," said Nadia, smiling back. "Okay, then. Thank you, Avery. It was nice having this meeting with you. I feel a lot better."

"Good," Avery said. With that, she stepped toward the door and she opened it up. Nadia gathered her things and then came around the table, making her way toward the exit.

"So I'll talk to you in a few days," said Nadia. "I'll make sure I have everything in order that you may want to discuss. Not that I don't have the account in order. But I'll just… yeah, I'll talk to you then."

"Thank you, Nadia," said Avery, bowing her head slightly, still standing at the open door.

After a moment of uncertainty, Nadia took Avery's cue and she exited first. When she looked behind her, Avery was still standing at the door and smiling. Nadia smiled back and then she picked up her feet, walking down the hallway back toward her office, wondering what had just happened. It wasn't what she had expected at all. It was a lot more pleasant and reassuring. Avery actually seemed like she could be a good boss. Maybe there really was nothing to worry about.

Nadia continued smiling as she walked away from the meeting. The image of Avery's beautiful face remained in her mind, however, and it made her feel pretty good.

WITH HER SLIM laptop open on an otherwise empty desk, Avery held her phone to her ear as she listened to the voice on the other end. She was speaking with Martin Shaw, the chief operating officer of Scheffler & Vonn, as he was in charge of overseeing the transition of Color Wheel from New York. Avery tapped her lip thoughtfully as Martin spoke.

"It doesn't make much sense to keep the company in Chicago long-term," said Martin. "It's moved beyond representing local clients, now heavily favoring national brands. If we absorb them and their clients, jettisoning any small local clients they have left, we can get exactly what we want out of the deal."

"The buy-out contract stipulates that we have to wait a year before making a move like that," said Avery. "And I must say, Martin, there are some pretty sharp people around here. The office is quite nice and it's well run."

"So we wait a year before we close it," said Martin. "Or we just get our lawyers involved to make sure we don't make any contractual mistakes. I'm sure we could keep the office running all while slowly moving the clients we want away from Color Wheel, and on to our own teams. If there's any talent there worth salvaging, we could send them to New York and bring them into our offices."

"This is what the board wants to do?" Avery asked.

"Yeah, this was the plan all along," said Martin. "You know that, Avery. Whenever some smaller upstart company has what you want, you just buy them and take your spoils. Those major clients are why we made this acquisition. Those are some huge contracts."

"We casually transition the big clients away, keeping them under the Color Wheel name," said Avery. "Until the waiting period is over and we can make more egregious moves."

"Yes," agreed Martin. "Hell, we could even open up a Color Wheel office in New York, in our building of course, so it all appears like the company is growing and doing well. And then, in a year's time, we simply absorb them into Scheffler & Vonn and we go on our merry way."

"Okay," said Avery coolly, fluffing her palm against her hair. "And what will become of me, Martin?"

"You?" Martin said. "Well, I'm sure there will be a position for you when you return. Paul is the acting chief administrative officer now, but we'll see where we're at in a year. It'll be up to the board. But I wouldn't worry about it. We all knew this would be a temporary assignment."

"Fine," Avery said. Moving her eyes to the open door of her office, she saw Frances approach with Laurie standing next to her. "Martin, let's reconnect on the plan in a couple of weeks. I've got a meeting."

"Will do," said Martin. "Thank you for the update, Avery. We'll touch base soon."

"Goodbye, Martin."

"Goodbye."

Avery set her phone down on her desk and smiled at her waiting guests.

"Come on in," Avery said, waving for them to approach. Frances and Laurie followed orders and walked together up to Avery's desk, sitting in the chairs in front of it.

"I don't know if I'll ever get used to sitting on this side of the desk," said Frances, offering a stilted laugh. Laurie smiled at her joke.

"I would think that side of the desk is more relaxing," said Avery. "Far fewer responsibilities. Especially in your case, Frances. What's the first move after you finish out your time with us?"

"My husband and I are going to Europe," said Frances. "We plan to spend three months traveling around, seeing historical sites."

"I think that sounds lovely," said Avery with a smile. "Now, what can I do for you ladies?"

"We put together the report you asked for," said Laurie. Removing a sheet of paper from a folder, she handed it over to Avery. Avery took the page and looked down into it. "This is our complete client list, ordered from highest yearly spend to lowest. We also noted which clients have on-going contracts with us, and which are on an as-needed basis."

"I see," said Avery. "This is all very clear, thank you."

"Many of these clients have been with Color Wheel

since the beginning," said Frances. "And some are even from my days as a freelancer, after I split with the agency I was working for and went my own way."

"I'm guessing those are some of these clients on the bottom," said Avery. "The clients that don't spend very much. Is that correct?"

"That's right," said Frances. "Despite our growth, we do still try to serve the clients who've been with us from the start."

"And it doesn't appear as though these clients pay the same rates as the larger clients," said Avery.

"Yes," said Frances. "They've been grandfathered into their rates."

"Have you ever discussed raising these rates with the clients themselves?" asked Avery. "Or have you just ignored that part of the equation to their benefit?"

"We've tried to remain fair," said Frances, looking over to Laurie who had a worried expression on her face. "And the smaller clients have had their rates raised in the past, but just not as steeply as the clients who can afford to pay more. The high end clients help subsidize the lower end clients."

"Some of these clients have very tiny ad budgets," interjected Laurie. "Just a couple thousand dollars per year. Nothing really. If we raised our rates any more, they would have to leave us and go with a cheaper agency or hire freelancers."

"Thank you," said Avery. "I understand. I'm very much interested in some of these clients at the top," she said, lightly tapping her finger on the paper before looking up at the two women. "Dizzy Harrison?"

"Dizzy Harrison is one of the clients I manage," said Laurie. "They're an internet eyeglass company. They sell inexpensive glasses. You send them your prescription and order a half dozen frames to try on at home. You pick the ones you want, they put it all together, and you can get your glasses for under a hundred dollars."

"And they spend a million a year in marketing?" Avery asked.

"They've grown in the last couple of years," said Laurie. "We do very well for them with internet and viral marketing. Some print, but not much."

"And Polly is at the top here," Avery continued.

"Polly has become our bread and butter," said Frances. "Their budget grows immensely every year."

"They are a premier brand," said Avery. She held up her own phone. "I myself have one."

"Yes, we all use their phones around here as well," said Frances. "So that they don't think we're cheating on them." She smiled warmly and Avery laughed.

"I'm going to study this list," Avery said with finality, setting the page down on her desk. "I appreciate the two of you putting this spreadsheet together for me. It certainly gives me a new view of the company overall."

"It's no problem at all, Avery," Frances said. "It's bittersweet for me. As I said, I've worked with some of those clients for a very long time."

"Laurie, if you could," Avery said.

"Yes?" said Laurie.

"Please breakdown for me the Dizzy Harrison account," said Avery. "I want to see where their money is going specifically and what things look like quarterly for them. Could you do that for me?"

"Of course," Laurie replied with a nod.

"Thank you," said Avery. "Now if you'll both excuse me, I have a call I need to make."

"Sure," said Frances. She smiled and stood up, and Laurie followed her lead. "Thank you, Avery. Let us know if you need anything further."

"I definitely will," said Avery. "Thank you again."

With a few more smiles and nods, Frances and Laurie took their leave from Avery's office, walking together through the doorway and making their way down the hall a few lengths before speaking. It was Laurie who spoke up first.

"I didn't get a good feeling about that," she said.

"Let's get a little further away from her office," Frances said in a whisper. They picked up their pace, and once she was sure they were out of earshot, Frances spoke again. "I'm with you on that. It was a little concerning to me."

"Right?" said Laurie. "I don't know what to think. It made me feel very exposed, having her dissect our clients like that."

"She is the boss now," admitted Frances. "And I'm sure she has the company's best interests at heart."

"I hope so," said Laurie. She paused and thought for a moment. "You said that it was built into the contract that

Scheffler & Vonn couldn't just swipe our clients away, right?"

"Yes," said Frances. "They have a year before they can make any major changes like that."

"A year?" Laurie repeated incredulously. "You didn't tell me that before."

"Well, yes," said Frances, almost as though she'd been caught in a lie. "But I wouldn't worry about it. They know that Color Wheel is highly successful. There's no need to mess with a good thing."

"I hope you're right," said Laurie.

"I am," Frances said, smiling to try to cheer Laurie up. "Don't worry about it. Let's just get back to work. You get Avery what she asked for, all right?"

"Yes, Frances," said Laurie. "I will."

"Good girl," Frances replied. She smiled once more, adjusted her glasses, and took off from Laurie, who was now left standing in front of her own office.

Laurie played out the meeting once again in her head, trying to remember all of what Avery had said. Her original positivity about Avery was melting away, and Laurie was beginning to worry that this transition might not work out how they had all believed it would.

Something wasn't quite right.

NADIA WALKED into the elevator with her bag hanging from her side. It had been a long week, and she was feeling

27

exhausted but good. She was proud of the work she did, no matter how hard it could be on certain days. Reaching out, she pressed the button to take her down to the building lobby.

"Hold that elevator, please," she heard a familiar voice say. Nadia reached out and stopped the doors from closing.

And then Avery appeared. She smiled when she saw that it was Nadia in the elevator.

"Why, hello," said Avery, stepping inside and standing next to Nadia. "Thank you, Nadia."

"No problem, Avery," she replied. Avery smoothed out her jacket and Nadia watched.

"Are you headed home?" Avery asked.

"Yes, I am," said Nadia. "I'm going to slip into something comfortable and pour myself a glass of wine."

"That does sound nice," said Avery. "But I was considering getting an afterwork cocktail at the restaurant in the building. Perhaps you'd join me?"

"Join you?" repeated Nadia. She was stunned. Of course it would be a good idea for her to have a drink with Avery. The closer she could get to her new boss, the more secure she knew she would be in her job.

"My treat," Avery continued on, offering Nadia another smile.

"Yes, absolutely," said Nadia."I'd like that."

"Terrific," said Avery. "Consider it thanks for your breakdown of the Polly account today. I have a much clearer vision of how things are working at Color Wheel and I'm quite enthused about it."

"Oh," said Nadia. "Sure. It's no problem."

"And if you happen to have one too many," Avery said wryly. "I'll be happy to order you a car home."

"Thank you," said Nadia. "But I don't live very far away. I often walk, especially when the weather's nice like it is today."

"If you can still walk," Avery quipped. "Then walk you shall." Nadia gave a small laugh.

"Okay," Nadia said. She smiled.

The restaurant on the ground floor of the building was large, open, and dark. Everything about it looked expensive, including the patrons. The downtown skyscraper in which Color Wheel called home was filled with many other successful Chicago businesses, including financial services firms, corporate offices for national brands, and insurance companies. The people who frequented the restaurant after-work most certainly had money. Avery fit right in, while Nadia felt a bit out of place.

"Should we sit at the bar?" Nadia asked gingerly, looking around the expansive restaurant as the ladies waited for the hostess to return.

"Don't be silly," said Avery. "We'll get a booth."

And get a booth they did. It was a large booth, large enough for six people, and Nadia felt almost like a child sitting there with so much space around her. But Avery seemingly filled her side of the booth. Not in physical space, as she was very fit, but in stature. There was something large about her. She commanded space.

After a bit of small talk, and the delivery of their drinks

— a gin and tonic for Avery, and a glass of red wine for Nadia — Avery developed a more calm face, she smiled, and she leaned in closer across the table from Nadia as though she were about to tell a secret.

"Nadia," said Avery. "You can relax. You seem very tense."

"Do I?" asked Nadia. "I'm sorry. I was just thinking that I've never actually been inside this place before. It always seemed like it wasn't for me."

"That's ridiculous," said Avery. "You work in the building. Of course it's for you. It's for anybody who comes in, really."

"That's not what I mean," said Nadia. "It's just... I know it's an expensive restaurant."

"I told you that it was my treat," countered Avery. "Don't worry about it."

"Yes, thank you," said Nadia.

"And I happen to know that you do quite well," said Avery. "You shouldn't worry about treating yourself to a place like this on occasion."

"You're right," said Nadia. "But that's new for me. My situation changed with my recent promotion, and I guess I haven't fully adjusted yet."

"You will," Avery assured her. She sipped delicately from the red straw in her drink.

"Yes," Nadia said, slowly nodding. She drank as well.

And then there was a moment of silence. Nadia still hadn't gotten over the awkwardness she felt about the situation. But she knew that she had to beat the anxiety. This kind of socializing was important to her career.

"So where are you staying while you're in town?" Nadia asked, trying to be casual.

"Oh, I've rented a penthouse suite in a newer building in Streeterville," said Avery. "It's very nice. Close to Michigan Avenue and the shops. It has a tremendous view of the lake."

"Do you think you'll stay there for a while?" Nadia said. "Not to pry to much, of course. I'm just wondering how it works for someone like you who had to move across the country for this job."

"It's fine," Avery assured her and smiled. "I do plan to stay in this building, as the cost is being covered by the company. I don't know how things will go ultimately, but I'm not worried about that right now."

Nadia smiled, sipped from her wine, and nodded at Avery. She could feel herself loosening up, and so she drank again. It helped her. Avery was such a beautiful woman, her blonde hair perfectly done, her blue eyes piercing and glimmering. She wore a black dress, conservative yet well-fitted to her figure. The desire within Nadia was growing, but she tried to hide it with a mundane conversation. It made her feel foolish to harbor an attraction to her boss.

"I have a loft condo," said Nadia. "In the West Loop. It's in an old chocolate factory and sometimes in summer you get this wonderfully faint aroma of chocolate. Maybe I'm just imagining it, it's so faint. But I love it."

"Mmm," hummed Avery, grinning contentedly. "I'd like to smell that. I'm a sucker for a good piece of chocolate."

Just then their waitress walked back and Avery ordered two more drinks with just a wave of her hand, no words necessary. Nadia watched Avery's confidence and she felt envious.

"Why don't you tell me about yourself?" Avery said, taking the last sip of her cocktail. "You're a very pretty woman and I don't see a ring on your finger." When she said this, Nadia looked to Avery's hand. Her finger was ring-less as well.

"Oh," Nadia said, looking to her one hand and turning it back and forth. And then, after a delay, she finally heard Avery's compliment and it brought a smile to her face. "Well, I suppose I've just put a lot of myself into my career and it's come at the expense of my love life."

"I can certainly relate to that," said Avery. "When you work as hard as women like us do, it's very difficult to find time for a relationship."

"Career was a dealbreaker in my last relationship," admitted Nadia, loosening up even further still. She noticed her wine glass was empty and she slid it to the edge of the table.

"Oh, how so?" Avery said with interest.

"Well, she and I—"

"*She*," repeated Avery, her eyes now afire and her smile getting bigger.

"Yes, she," said Nadia. "I'm—"

"Oh, I know," Avery said, interrupting yet again. "I knew right away."

Nadia's eyes grew wider and her heart really started to race. Looking across the table, there was something different in Avery's eyes, different than any expression Nadia had seen in her boss since meeting her. She looked like a hungry predator and it made Nadia feel like an agreeable prey.

"So, she and I…" Nadia went on. "We split because she had an amazing job offer in San Francisco. And I love my career here."

"Tell me about her," cooed Avery, deeply fascinated. "I'd really love to know about this woman."

"My ex?" said Nadia. "Well, her name is Lucy. She's kind of a hipster geek, very brilliant with technology. She has tattoos and piercings and—"

"Anything *interesting* pierced?" asked Avery. The waitress then ambled up to their table and delivered their drinks, while both women looked up to her and thanked her. Nadia, however, couldn't quite suppress her growing arousal from Avery's questioning and her voice cracked slightly.

"I, um…" said Nadia, looking back to Avery after the waitress disappeared.

"She did, didn't she?"

"She had her nipples pierced," Nadia admitted after a beat. She immediately felt embarrassed.

"Both?" said Avery.

"Yes," said Nadia. She couldn't believe she was divulging so much, but Avery had some uncanny ability to pull this information out of her. "Barbells."

"That's so hot, isn't it?" said Avery. She shivered and laughed, and then picked up her fresh cocktail and sipped.

"Well, yeah," said Nadia. "Yeah, I thought it was pretty hot."

"Nadia," said Avery with seduction in her voice. Nadia looked down and saw that Avery had put her foot, which she had removed from her shoe, on the booth seat right next to Nadia's leg. "What do you say we order a little bite to eat? Some food, a little more wine. Let's make a date of it."

"I... sure," said Nadia, her smile growing despite the nervousness she felt. "I'd like that."

"Great," said Avery.

Avery grinned, and Nadia could feel it all throughout her body.

THEY WERE BOTH LAUGHING. As Nadia and Avery stumbled together up to Nadia's door, their conversation was animated and boisterous. It was obvious they'd both drunk their share. Nadia fumbled with her bag, trying to find her keys, feeling like she was ready to get out of her work clothes. Avery, meanwhile, stood behind her, looked around the cavernous hallway with its steel and wood supports, and she sniffed in the air.

"I still don't smell chocolate, Nadia," said Avery, serious about her assertion. "I was told there would be fragrances of chocolate."

"No," Nadia countered with a laugh. "I told you that

sometimes in summer, when it's much warmer, I *believe* I can smell chocolate. It's probably just all in my head." She laughed again, pushed her key into the lock, and opened up the door. The two women spilled inside together, and Nadia shut the door behind them.

Avery confidently strolled into the kitchen, and she searched around until she found an unopened bottle of wine tucked back on the counter next to the refrigerator. As Nadia took off her shoes, dropped her bag, and fulfilled her post-work routine, she watched as Avery made herself at home, opening the bottle up and pouring two glasses full.

"This is a lovely place," Avery said, handing a glass to Nadia.

"Thank you," Nadia replied.

"Very high ceilings," remarked Avery.

"Yes," said Nadia. "It's actually not a very large space, but the ceilings make it look bigger than it is."

"Indeed," said Avery. She smiled and took a sip.

Nadia removed her jacket, leaving her standing there in the matching pants and a sleeveless blouse, and she tossed it over back of one of the barstools next to the kitchen island. She wanted to change, to dress down for the night, but that felt like it would be a strange move with Avery present. So she just smiled, drank from her glass, and watched as Avery summarized her condo.

"This is very much the style right now, isn't it?" asked Avery. "The modern timber loft?"

"Yes," said Nadia. "I guess it is sort of in fashion."

"I've certainly seen the imagery in design magazines,"

said Avery. "My taste is a little more modern. Dark grey, stainless steel, clean lines."

"That's nice, too," said Nadia. "You know," she said, her demeanor changing slightly. "Don't feel you have to stay very long if you need to get home."

"Oh, nonsense," Avery quickly said. "Are you not enjoying my presence?"

"No, I am," said Nadia. She paused, she looked to Avery, absorbing her beauty, and she smiled. "I'm happy you're here."

"Good," said Avery, stepping further into the condo, toward the seating area now. "I'm happy to be here, as well. It's difficult being new to a city and not having your usual social outlets."

Avery sat herself down on the couch as Nadia followed her into the living room. She considered for a moment that she might sit on the chair opposite the couch, but instead decided to take a seat next to her boss. It felt nice to be next to her.

"You don't know anyone in Chicago?" asked Nadia. "I find that difficult to believe."

"Oh, I know some people," said Avery. "Of course. But they aren't always that fun, and I'm the kind of woman who likes to have a lot of fun."

"You are?"

"I am," Avery said. She grinned. "Do you think something about my exterior purports otherwise?"

"I... no," said Nadia. "I don't think that at all."

"Or maybe because I'm the boss," said Avery. "Of a high-class pedigree from the east coast?"

"No," Nadia said again, now laughing nervously. "I don't think that. I don't."

"Because having fun is my *raison d'être*," Avery said with her smile wide and her wine glass hoisted aloft. "What's the point of success if you can't enjoy it?"

"I'll drink to that," teased Nadia. She raised her glass and then drank from it. Avery followed suit.

"When you work hard, I find you also need to play hard," said Avery. "To achieve balance. Otherwise, life becomes dull."

"That's easy enough to say when you can have anything you want," said Nadia, immediately feeling embarrassed and putting her hand over her mouth. Avery, however, laughed joyously.

"I think you have it all wrong, darling," Avery said, a familiar fire dancing in her eyes. "When you can have anything you want, you begin to lust after things that are a bit more difficult to obtain. Things that money can't always buy."

"Like what?" Nadia asked quietly, though she felt as though she had an inkling of the answer. Avery laughed, obviously tickled by the conversation.

Avery leaned forward and sat her half-full wine glass on the coffee table, and then she eased back into the couch, turned toward Nadia, smiling contentedly the entire time. Her blue eyes flashed, her skin was creamy and smooth, yet it did tell a story about her age. Avery's looks were the product of natural beauty partnered with money. Nadia couldn't deny her attraction to her boss, no matter how hard she tried to force it from her mind.

As though she could read Nadia's mind, Avery laughed once again.

"Nadia," Avery began, smiling at Nadia with their faces only about a foot or so apart. She reached up and delicately fingered Nadia's hair. "I find you to be an attractive young woman. You have a pretty face, a terrific body, and a smart mind. As I said, the people I know here in Chicago... they aren't the kind of people that I can rely on for the kind of... *socialization* that I enjoy."

"Well, I——"

Avery interrupted her by tenderly holding a single finger to Nadia's lips.

"Don't interrupt someone when they're complimenting you," asserted Avery. "Now, as I was saying. I find you to be very attractive, and I very much enjoy attractive women. I enjoy spending time with them, particularly at night. Do you understand?"

"I think I do."

"Of course you do," said Avery. "Do you find me attractive?"

Nadia, as though she were in a trance, slowly nodded her head. Avery's grin grew larger.

"Do you want to kiss me?" asked Avery in a whisper.

"Yes," intoned Nadia.

"I give you my consent," said Avery. "You can kiss me anywhere you like."

Nadia took a deep breath, her nerves causing her a slight tremor. She felt like her heart could leap out of her chest. The exchange with Avery had gone from playful to erotic very quickly, and something else inside of Nadia was beginning to take over. Something vigorously carnal.

Without another thought, Nadia leaned in and pressed her lips to Avery's, and Avery accepted them with a soft moan. The kiss grew in intensity rather quickly, with hands moving, breaths hastening, and desire mounting. No longer did Avery represent her job, rather she was now an object of lust for Nadia. She was eager for the touch of another, as it had been far too long.

It might have been the blurring of time from the quantities of alcohol the women had drank, but things moved swiftly. Before Nadia knew it, she and Avery were in her bedroom, tearing their clothing off in-between kisses and gropes, until they tumbled down into the bed together and intertwined their nude bodies. Nadia was already sweating in anticipation, and she was unable to keep the sounds escaping her mouth as Avery touched her between her legs.

At one point, with Nadia lying back into the cushion of her pillows, Avery rested lower down on Nadia's body, playing with her breasts, and sucking on her nipples. She would wrap her hands around either side of one of Nadia's tits, offering it a tender squeeze, and then suck and nibble tenderly. It made Nadia's head spin, and she made her passion known with low moans oozing out of her parted lips.

In a random moment of sober clarity amid their inebriated intercourse, with Avery's fingers penetrating her, Nadia laughed to herself as she realized that she was in bed with her boss. There could be repercussions to this, surely, but she couldn't bring herself to care. Instead, Nadia meditated on the pressured thrusting, wondering how Avery was so expertly able to play just the right notes, and she held on to herself tightly, wishing for it to never end.

Sometime within the sixty-nine position, Avery hanging over top with her face pressed deeply between Nadia's legs, Nadia dropped her head to the pillow and stared upward. The reflexive fervor was beginning to overtake her, her left foot kicking just slightly and of its own accord. She focused her eyes on Avery's middle, admiring the perfectly mani-cured blonde bush, lips damp from Nadia's previous efforts. And then Nadia was coming. She shook and vibrated, her mouth agape and releasing groans out into the otherwise quiet bedroom. But Avery did not stop. Nadia's obvious orgasm only made Avery work harder.

After it was all over, the women lying there together, panting and trying to regain their composure, Nadia felt absolutely giddy. She was still feeling pickled from the drink, but it made her feel free. The romp with Avery was the best sex she had ever experienced, and she might have said that out loud. She wasn't sure, though, immediately after the thought came to her whether or not she'd vocalized it. No matter. Nadia lay there buzzing, feeling the cool sweat evap-orate off her exposed flesh, laughing with Avery over words that Nadia could not remember being spoken.

In fact, she couldn't remember very much at all. She

only knew what she felt. And what she felt was fulfillment, wonder, acceptance, and completion. Most of all, she felt deep affection. And it brought a big smile to Nadia's face.

When the morning light began to shine in through her bedroom window, stirring her from sleep, Nadia stretched her arms upward, her breasts coming uncovered from the thin sheet that lay over top of her. She smiled as she opened her eyes, feeling slightly hungover, but quite sure of what had happened the previous evening. When she turned over and looked to the other side of the bed, however, it was empty.

She was alone.

———

THE NEXT DAY WAS A SATURDAY. Nadia had felt somewhat abandoned when she woke up to discover that Avery had left, and the note left for her on the kitchen counter didn't make it much better. In a flowing script handwriting, Avery had thanked her for the nice time, proposed they do it again sometime, and asked that Nadia remain discreet. It felt like a transaction. But Nadia couldn't quite reconcile these feelings with the growing desire she felt for her boss.

It was confusing.

Nadia showered and dressed, getting going for the day much earlier than she usually did. She walked down the building hallway with urgency, turned a corner, and walked a little further. Approaching a door, she gave it a hurried knock and then she waited.

There was some commotion on the other side of the door, then there was silence. After a moment, the door swung open and Laurie stood there with a sleepy smile on her face, standing in her pajamas.

"Good morning," Laurie said. "You're up and at 'em pretty early today."

"Yeah," Nadia said absentmindedly, looking down at herself and then back to her friend. "I just felt like I needed to get moving, I guess."

"My coffeemaker just finished," Laurie said, thumbing back inside her condo. "Would you like a cup?"

"Definitely," said Nadia.

The morning sun shone brightly inside of Laurie's condo, and the two women sat opposite each other in comfortable chairs with a small table between them near the door to Laurie's porch. Laurie sat with one foot up on the chair, an arm wrapped around it to pull it close, while she sipped from her mug. Nadia leaned forward in her chair, hovering over the table, as she stared down into her creamy coffee.

"So that's where you were," Laurie said, slowly nodding as she absorbed the tale Nadia had woven for her. "When I got home last night, I stopped by your place to see if you wanted to get a drink with me and Tara from upstairs. But you were out."

"Unexpectedly," said Nadia. "And I had such a nice time, you know? I don't really do that. Go out for drinks and then hop into bed. You know that's not my style."

"I know," said Laurie.

"And with her leaving sometime in the night," Nadia continued. "It just feels so sordid."

"I didn't mention this to you," said Laurie. "But I had this short meeting the other day with Avery and Frances. And I just really got this bad feeling from Avery. I can't put my finger on it, but it felt like she had some ulterior motives that she was hiding."

"I think she's very complex," said Nadia. "Last night, when we were out, she was a different Avery than what I was used to in the office. We had a lot of fun. At first, I was pretty anxious about it. It felt awkward. But once I loosened up, I really felt at ease. I mean, obviously I did if I ended up having sex with her."

"Maybe she just doesn't want it to be weird at work," Laurie posited.

"Well, leaving in the middle of the night isn't the thing to do if you're trying to keep it from being weird," countered Nadia.

"True," said Laurie.

"And now I feel like a fool," said Nadia. "Because I think I actually like her."

"It might have just been a one night stand to her," said Laurie. "You need to consider that."

"That could be," Nadia said. "But wouldn't that be a messed up thing to do with a work colleague. With an *employee*."

"I'm just as confused as you are," said Laurie. "I think you just need to ask her point blank. You need to find out what's going on."

"I honestly don't know what to expect at this point," said Nadia. "Last night, when she started coming on to me, I was completely blown away. I couldn't believe someone as beautiful and successful would be interested in me."

"What are you talking about?" said Laurie swiftly. "You're an amazing woman, Nadia. You're gorgeous, you're smart, you're successful, too."

"Not like her," said Nadia.

"In a different way," said Laurie. "And anyways, she's just where she is because of where she comes from. She was born into her position. Not to say Avery hasn't also worked hard, but she was born way ahead of us."

Nadia considered her friend's words, and she sipped her coffee slowly. The warmth of the drink made her feel really comforted.

"Just because Avery is more upper class than you," Laurie went on. "That doesn't mean she can't also be legitimately interested in you. Thinking otherwise is just selling yourself short."

"It was so good, too," said Nadia, eyes glazing over as she remembered. "Wow. Some of the best sex I've ever had."

"Oh boy," Laurie said with a laugh. "I really don't need to know any of the details."

"She's a pro, Laurie," Nadia continued. "I remember at one point I was staring into her glistening—"

"Nadia!" said Laurie, laughing again. "No!"

"Sorry," said Nadia, letting out a nervous laugh. "It was just great."

"I get that."

"I guess I don't want this to be it," said Nadia. "I don't want it to be just a one night stand. I really want to get to know her."

"I'd like to know more about her, too," said Laurie. "At work, she really confuses me. She *seems* friendly, but then she also seems like she's hiding something. Like maybe she's a secret plotting bitch. I don't know. But she can put on a really convincing face and I even find myself smitten with her."

"That's what I mean," said Nadia. "I think she's complex. I think there's something else going on and I'm not sure what it is."

"I'd really like to know," said Laurie. "Because no matter what Frances says or what Avery says, I'm still fearing for my job. I'm still really uncertain about how this buy-out is going to affect us in the long run."

"Me too," admitted Nadia. "I don't feel settled about it at all."

"Maybe you're in a position to figure this all out for us," said Laurie. "From the *inside*."

"Is that a sex joke?" Nadia asked knowingly.

"It is."

"Well, I'll poke around and see if I can make her come," said Nadia. "Come clean, that is." They both laughed.

"You're smiling now," said Laurie happily.

"I feel a lot better about this," said Nadia. "I was really confused this morning, and hurt. But there's so much more to this that I don't even know. And I think it could be really exciting to figure it out. Provided, of course, it wasn't just some one night stand, or that Avery will ignore me come Monday, or that she might just fold Color Wheel up and send us packing."

"Yeah, that would be the worst case scenario," said Laurie. "It's rarely the worst case scenario."

"Do you think it's a bad idea to try to pursue some kind of romance with your boss?" asked Nadia. "Even if she's sexy and rich and powerful?"

"Yeah, I think it generally is," said Laurie in faux-seriousness. The friends laughed together once again.

"I'm such an idiot, aren't I?" said Nadia, putting her hand to her forehead and shaking her head gently.

"You're not," said Laurie. "Really, you're not. This stuff is just complicated. It's what makes life exciting, in my opinion."

"Right," said Nadia. She paused for a moment, lost in thought. "I'm going to go."

"Okay," said Laurie, offering an accepting smile. "I won't tell anybody about this."

"Thank you," said Nadia. "I appreciate that."

"But if you find out what's going on," said Laurie, wagging a finger. "I need to know. Work has gotten so disconcerting and I'd really like a head's up if I have to get my resume together."

"I don't think it's going to come to that," Nadia replied.

"Are you sure?"

"I'm not sure," said Nadia.

"Exactly," said Laurie. She stood up, and then Nadia

stood up as well. The friends stepped closer to one another and embraced tightly, lingering there in silence for a moment as Laurie tenderly rubbed Nadia's back.

"Thanks for being a great friend," said Nadia.

"Any time," said Laurie.

Standing in the open door of Laurie's condo, the women hugged once more. Nadia's anxiety had abated with Laurie's help, and she was grateful. But she knew she had a lot more to think about before confronting Avery on Monday. It was certain to be a long weekend, lost in thought, playing out scenarios in her head. Lucky that she had a great friend living just down the hall.

As Nadia made her way back to her own condo, she couldn't help but think about the night that she and Avery had spent together. The details were all coming back to her. It had been a pretty hot time, and as Nadia continued to play back the tape in her mind, she could feel her heart begin to beat faster. She smiled deeply.

"THAT'S A VERY GOOD QUESTION, MEGHAN," said Avery, standing at the head of the table in the conference room. The chairs were filled with the usual suspects. Frances sat to Avery's side, Nadia and Laurie were a few chairs away. "I think, if your research is correct, then increasing the budget for YouTube advertisement would certainly be in the client's best interest."

"Thank you, Avery," said Meghan, scribbling a note down on the paper in front of her.

"You're welcome," Avery replied. "Now, unless there are any more questions, I think we can bring this Monday morning meeting to a close." She paused and looked around the room. After a moment, Avery smiled. "Thank you, all. Let's have a productive week."

The employees began standing up, making a commotion as they collected their things and made their way toward the exit. Nadia and Laurie stood up together.

"You go ahead," said Nadia in a slight whisper. "I'm going to stay and talk to Avery."

"Good luck," said Laurie, giving Nadia's arm a squeeze. Nadia replied with a smile.

Nadia clutched her notebook and ambled toward Avery, who was standing alongside Frances, the two of them having an open conversation about the continuing transition. As Nadia neared, the rest of the others had departed and now it was only the three of them left in the conference room. Both Avery and Frances turned to Nadia, giving her their attention as she sidled up next to them.

"Excuse me," said Nadia. "I'm not interrupting, am I?"

"Of course not, dear," said Frances with a warm smile.

"Thank you," said Nadia. "I was wondering if I could speak with Avery privately?" When she said this, Avery's eyes lit up and a curious smile curled over her lips.

"Kicking me out, is that it?" teased Frances. "It's like I don't even work here anymore."

"Oh, Frances," said Nadia quickly. "I didn't mean to—"

"Relax, Nadia," said Frances. "I'm just teasing. Avery, we'll just continue this conversation later. You deal with this one."

"That's fine," said Avery, offering a single nod to Frances.

"Oh, and Nadia," said Frances. "I want to speak with you about a Polly matter when you have a moment. Just stop by my office."

"Yes, Frances," said Nadia. "I will."

"Thank you," said Frances. She gave one more smile and then sauntered off toward the door.

Avery looked on at Nadia in silence, still with a curious and amused expression, waiting as though she were giving Nadia the floor to speak first. Nadia waited for a moment in uncertainty before she opened her mouth and went for it.

"I had a good time with you on Friday night," said Nadia with hope in her eyes. She was nervous. It made her feel much younger, much less experienced, to be having this conversation.

"I did as well," said Avery evenly, still yielding the conversation, still smiling.

"I didn't expect things to happen like they did," said Nadia. "But... I had fun. I enjoyed it."

"You're very talented in bed," said Avery with a matter-of-fact tone. "That tongue of yours is a lethal weapon." Nadia could feel herself blushing from Avery's frankness, a light sweat coming to her under her arms and behind her knees.

"That's... thank you," Nadia said, not knowing how to

take such a compliment from someone like Avery. "I really enjoyed your abilities as well."

"I suppose you're wondering why I left," said Avery.

"I am."

"As I said in my note," Avery began. "Discretion is very important. And when you informed me that one of our coworkers lives in your building, I decided it would be in our best interest that I not depart from your condo during a time that she might be around to see. It would look bad, you understand."

"Yes," said Nadia, nodding slowly as she thought about what Avery said. "I suppose that's right."

"It wouldn't look good for the boss to be seen leaving an employee's home," Avery reiterated. "Hair a mess, wearing yesterday's clothing. It might cause gossip. Or worse, ill feelings. You might be suspected of receiving special treatment by your coworkers, Nadia, if they found out that we had been intimate. You haven't told anyone, have you?"

"I haven't," Nadia said, averting her eyes.

"Good," said Avery. "Let's just keep this between us. And we can see what develops." Avery's grin grew bigger.

"This is all pretty confusing to me, I must admit," said Nadia. "I spent the entire weekend trying to figure it out. I wasn't really sure how you felt."

"Listen," Avery said. She reached up and delicately fondled a tendril of Nadia's hair. "Don't think too hard about it. Let's have fun. But let's keep it out of the office. It will be our thing. They needn't know. It's none of their business, anyway."

"So, do you want to *date* me or—"

"Nadia," said Avery with authority. "That big analytical brain of yours is going to be your undoing. Don't overthink it." Avery looked over Nadia's shoulder toward the door and, reassured that they were alone, she leaned in closer to Nadia's ear and spoke in a whisper. "Do you want to feel my tongue again in your softest, wettest places?"

"Very much."

"Do you remember when I licked you completely?" Avery asked, still in a hushed tone. "Front to back."

"Yes."

"Would you like to feel that again?"

"Definitely," said Nadia. Her heart was racing, and she could feel herself getting turned on right there in the conference room.

"Then don't overthink it," Avery said. "Don't overthink it and you can do anything you want to me. You can tell me what you like and I'll do it. If you haven't deduced by now, I quite enjoy sex and I'm very taken by you." Avery touched Nadia's chin lightly. "So let's have fun together."

"Okay," Nadia said softly. "Let's have fun."

"Good," said Avery, standing up straight and proper once more, her voice returning to normal. "I'm glad that we're in agreement."

Nadia nodded, trying to calm herself. But Avery's words and her authority had made Nadia hot. She felt flushed and excited. It was a strange feeling for her at work.

"Now, if there's nothing else," said Avery. "We should both probably get back to work."

"All right," said Nadia. "Will I see you soon?"

"You will."

"Great," she said. Nadia looked around for a moment and then took a deep breath. "Thank you, Avery."

"Thank you, Nadia."

Nadia remained standing there in silence for a moment longer, while Avery just smiled. Then Nadia gave another nod and she turned from her boss, quickly scurrying out of the conference room while Avery watched her exit. Even though Nadia couldn't see it, Avery blew her a kiss as she left.

Sitting alone in her office, with her door closed, Nadia focused on her breathing and tried to calm herself. But her heart was beating fast and her middle ached. It was completely silent in her office but for the sounds of her labored breathing. Never had she been this aroused for a woman, never had she been so excited for the promise of sex. But Avery was a completely different proposition than what she was accustomed to. And that Avery wanted to keep it secret made the tryst all the more alluring.

Without thinking about where she was, Nadia quickly unclipped the waist of her dress slacks and plunged her hand down inside. She pushed a finger against the tensile fabric of her underwear and delicately dragged it forward. Then, removing her hand from her pants, she brought her finger up so she could see it. Her fingertip was wet and glistening in the fluorescent light of her office. She was so turned on, she had soaked through.

Just as she started to weigh the options of touching

herself right there in her office to release the pressure, intensely sexual thoughts of Avery bounding through her mind's eye, she was broken from her lustful reverie by the jarring sound of her phone ringing. It startled Nadia, she made a sound of surprise, and she jumped in her chair. It was a stark reminder of where she was.

Reaching over, she grabbed her desk phone, wrapping her fingers around it and almost simultaneously realizing that she had smeared some of her own wetness on the handset. She chastised herself internally, but then quickly turned her attention to the caller.

"Hello?" she said. "This is Nadia."

"So how did it go?" asked Laurie in a secretive whisper. "Did it all work out like you'd hoped?"

"Laurie," Nadia said in relief, thankful that it was her friend and not a client. "I don't think I can talk about it here. But it went well. It went really well."

"You'll have to tell me all about it," said Laurie. "I want every detail."

"I don't think you do."

"Oh, I do."

"Okay," said Nadia. "I'll tell you tonight over some wine."

"Goodie," Laurie replied, her own excitement apparent over the phone.

"I can't talk right now, though," said Nadia. She looked down to her unbuttoned slacks and questioned the thoughts that were coming to her. "I've got to... get to work."

"Okay," said Laurie. "We'll catch up later, then. I'm excited, Nadia. I'm really excited about this."

"I'm excited, too."

NADIA GROANED out in pleasure and she opened her eyes to look down the length of her nude body. She was splayed out on Avery's bed, buoyant atop fluffy white bed linens, while Avery perched between her legs. Avery held a thick blue silicon toy and was firmly and methodically penetrating Nadia with it, while using the thumb of her opposite hand to rub Nadia's clit in steady circles. It was making Nadia's head spin.

With her lust-drunk eyes focused on Avery, Nadia looked over her lover's body. Her apple-sized breasts bounced with elasticity as she pleasured Nadia. She was fit and slim, yet muscular in her arms and stomach. Avery's face had a subtle glimmer of perspiration, and just above her forehead her blonde hair looked slightly matted down. Her cheeks were pink. When Avery's blue eyes darted up from her work and caught Nadia's eyes, she smiled. And Nadia smiled as well.

"You like this?" Avery said, massaging Nadia's clit with greater vigor, before swiftly lowering her head and licking it with similar enthusiasm. Nadia squirmed and moaned.

"Oh, I love it," she replied. "I really love it."

Avery thrust the toy deep inside of Nadia, and Nadia could feel the wonderful pressure of it. With her lips around Nadia's clit, Avery left the silicone piece inside and Nadia couldn't help but reflexively squeeze onto it. It felt wonderful. Her head rolled on the pillows.

The next thing Nadia knew they had changed gears, and Avery had mounted her and was bracing herself on Nadia's knee. Nadia's foot pressed deeply into the bed as Avery forcefully grinded into her, their wet heat rubbing back and forth against each other. Avery was breathing hard, and in this position Nadia could see Avery's abdominal muscles clenching. To Nadia, it almost felt like the room was spinning. It was as though she were drunk on sex.

Nadia had lost count of her orgasms. It had to have been at least three, but it could have been four. And with Avery at the helm, it felt as though another one could come on at any moment. It was like nothing Nadia had ever experienced before.

During a break in the festivities, Nadia laid alone in bed trying to catch her breath. Sprawled out naked, with one hand on her upper chest, feeling the rise and fall, feeling her heart race within. She was tingling, almost numb in places, like her body was losing sensation due to the sensation overload it had been subjected to. There was a sly smile on Nadia's face. She was happy.

After a moment, Avery trotted back into the bedroom holding two glasses of water. She, too, was still completely in the buff, and when Nadia saw her naked beauty, her heart melted and she smiled warmly. Avery approached the bed, sat down next to Nadia, and handed over a glass as Nadia slowly sat up.

"Thank you," said Nadia, immediately taking a drink. She sighed in refreshment. "That's good."

"We both needed a drink," Avery affirmed, she too sipping from her glass. She then set it down on the nightstand. "You're not finished, are you?"

"No," huffed Nadia happily. "No, I could go again." She took another drink, and then also put her water on the nightstand.

"I'm just so turned on seeing you like this," Avery said, looking up and down Nadia's body, admiring her. She delicately traced her fingers through the fur between Nadia's legs. "I can't help myself."

Nadia could feel the adoration coming from Avery, and it made her happy. The joy of feeling wanted showed in her face.

"I have to admit," said Nadia, feeling a bit embarrassed by her feelings but letting them out nonetheless. "I don't think I've ever had better sex than this."

"Oh, you poor girl," teased Avery, her fingers still lightly grazing back and forth over Nadia's bush. "So many years wasted." Nadia laughed softly.

"I mean, I've had plenty of *good* sex," corrected Nadia. "But being with you, it's like in a completely different league."

"I've had plenty of practice," said Avery with a grin. "And it also helps that I'm a perfectionist. Why do something at all if you don't try to do it perfectly?"

"You don't half-ass anything, do you?" asked Nadia.

"Not if I can help it," said Avery. "You know, I will tell you the secret to good sex."

"I'm listening," Nadia said, smiling contentedly.

"It's to be open to things," said Avery. "To try something new. To allow yourself to be free from judgment, and to not judge your partner. You may not like everything you try, but you have to *really* try to know. You have to give yourself over completely. Otherwise, you will become stuck in the same old predictable patterns."

"There's something I've always wanted to try," Nadia said gently with bashfulness in her tone.

"Tell me," replied Avery, her eyes lighting up. She looked down at Nadia with glee and excitement.

"I don't know," said Nadia. "It feels silly."

"It's not silly," asserted Avery. "I would love to know what it is."

"Well," said Nadia cautiously. "All right. I guess I've always wondered what it would be like to be fucked with a strap-on."

"You've never done that?" Avery asked with incredulousness.

"No," said Nadia. She laughed and then covered her face. "I can't believe I said that."

"Oh, Nadia," said Avery. "You're missing out." She held a single finger up for a moment, paused, and then got a disappointed look on her face. "You know, if we were at my condo in New York I could make your dreams a reality tonight. But this is a rental and I have very few of my things here."

"Avery, it's okay," Nadia said, reaching out for her hand and holding it tightly. "I shouldn't have said anything."

"I don't want you to worry,"Avery said, her eyes looking upwards as she thought. "I'll make this happen for you."

"No, it's okay," Nadia said again. "Really."

Avery simply looked down at Nadia and smiled deeply. It was in that moment that Nadia really felt as though there was something between them that was more than just sex. The expression on Avery's face made Nadia feel as though she was very interested in making her happy.

The lovers went for another tumble in the sheets. Nadia was quickly buzzing again, easily aroused by Avery's attentiveness and skill. It seemed as though Avery herself was most turned on when she was giving love, rather than when she was receiving. She liked control, and she liked to lead the charge. And Nadia loved to be dominated, she treasured a lover who knew her way around and wasn't afraid of going for it. The two women were a perfect match in the bedroom, and Nadia could feel her affection easily growing for Avery.

At one point, with Nadia's face buried into the pillows, her ass up in the air as she perched on her knees, she felt a wave of intensity begin to foment inside of her. Avery was sitting behind her, face between Nadia's ass cheeks, her tongue exploring from behind, while her hand moved back and forth over Nadia's pussy. Two fingers slipped between Nadia's wet lips, massaging over Nadia's clit with each gesture. It was a sensation that Nadia had never felt before, and it was magical.

Nadia clenched. Her knees were growing weaker and her body began to jerk. She was coming and she no longer felt in control of herself. After a few lustful moans, the tingling sensations began to tickle and Nadia started laughing. It was more like giggling, uncontrollable giggling. She twitched and spasmed, still laughing, until she fell over on the bed and dissolved into her orgasm. Opening her eyes and looking back at Avery, she saw her lover grinning at her and wiping at her own mouth with the back of her hand.

Later on, Nadia stood on the balcony of Avery's condo wearing a short silk robe, cream colored with black trim and a matching silk belt, staring out at the vastness of Lake Michigan. It was dark, probably around ten at night, yet various city lights illuminated the vantage. Nadia could see the lights just below Avery's building at Navy Peer and she could see the lights on the docks in the harbor just a bit south. It was a tremendous, expensive view.

Avery moved onto the balcony from behind Nadia, and she carried with her two glasses of red wine. Nadia smiled delicately as she accepted one of the glasses. Avery returned the smile easily. She was dressed in the very same silk robe as Nadia. It was loose and comfortable, very luxurious feeling, yet sexy and revealing as it only came down to mid-thigh.

"Thank you," said Nadia, taking a drink. "This view is incredible."

"It certainly is," said Avery. She stepped up to the railing alongside Nadia and looked out at the lake. "In a way, it reminds me of looking out at the Atlantic in New York. It goes on forever."

"The third coast," mused Nadia.

"It feels like it," Avery replied.

"Avery," said Nadia carefully, turning to her side and leaning on the railing, cradling her wine glass. "This is wonderful."

"It is, isn't it?" said Avery with a keen smile.

"I mean, I really enjoy our time together," said Nadia. "I'm smitten."

Avery maintained her smile and nodded knowingly.

"This isn't just sex, is it?" Nadia asked. There was a small tremor in her voice.

Reaching out, Avery ran her fingers delicately along Nadia's cheek and her smile grew slightly sad. It was though she knew something that Nadia didn't. The expression didn't sit well with Nadia. It confused her all the more.

"I like you," Avery said after a moment. "Nadia, you are a very wonderful woman and even though I haven't known you very long, I can sense that you're a good person. And I'm certainly very attracted to you. *Very*."

Nadia smiled demurely and looked away.

"Things are complex for me, however," Avery said after another pause. Nadia felt her smile drain away. "I don't know if I can make any promises, you see. I'm here in Chicago for one reason, and that is to absorb Color Wheel into Scheffler & Vonn."

"Absorb?" asked Nadia with new curiosity. "What do you mean?"

"Oh, you know," Avery replied with a stammer, almost

like she was backtracking. "To bring Color Wheel into the family. To take ownership of our new acquisition."

"Is that all you mean?"

Avery looked on at Nadia and Nadia could see the guard drop in her lover's face. What had been hardened and self-assured in Avery, was now more fragile and uncertain. She paused, she drank from her glass, and then Avery returned her eyes to Nadia with a new expression of honesty.

"The plan is to completely take over Color Wheel," said Avery. "To absorb the company's clients, and to eventually wind it down."

"You're kidding," said Nadia, feeling as though she'd just been smacked. She was dumbfounded. Stepping back from the balcony railing, she set her glass down on a small wrought-iron table and let it sink in. Placing her hand on her cheek, Nadia wasn't sure how to feel.

"Nadia," said Avery with a renewed authority. "This is between us, all right? I'm only telling you because I care, because I do have feelings for you, and I want you to understand how complex this situation is. How do you think I feel?"

But Nadia was feeling sick. Reconciling the affection she was feeling for Avery with Avery's corporate mission proved to be too much in the moment. She felt dizzy.

"I think I need to go," Nadia said finally. "I think I need to go home."

"I understand," Avery said with disappointment in her eyes. "I'll call you a car."

Avery turned from Nadia, holding her wine glass aloft,

and she disappeared back inside the condo. The sound of waves rolling into shore could be heard in the distance. Nadia continued standing there on the balcony, a cool wind coming in off of the lake, her eyes staring out in the darkness.

TWO

*N*adia sat at the small wooden table opposite Laurie. The restaurant, itself mostly decorated with reclaimed wood, vintage lighting, and tin ceilings, was a popular spot for brunch and the sound of conversation was all around. The friends each had a bloody mary in front of them, with a single plate of beignets in the center of the table. Laurie looked animated and happy, while Nadia had slight disappointment in her eyes.

It was Sunday, and it had only been a couple days since Nadia left Avery. She was feeling remorse for what she'd done, despite the circumstances. But she was becoming resigned to the fact that it was just a quick romance, something that probably shouldn't have happened, and something that she would just have to get over as she processed what might come next for her.

"These beignets are awesome," said Laurie, picking one

of the small doughnuts up and popping it into her mouth. She chewed and grinned. Nadia offered a small laugh.

"This place is known for them," Nadia remarked. She sipped from her drink through the straw.

"So," Laurie went on, dusting some powdered sugar off of her fingertips. "You've got to tell me how your date with you-know-who went on Friday. I'm dying to know."

"I don't know," said Nadia. "I'm just not sure it's going anywhere."

"Really?" asked Laurie. "What makes you say that?"

"Maybe we're just too different," Nadia replied. "I'm not sure. I think it's just going to fizzle out."

"You're kidding me," said Laurie. "What about what she said to you after the meeting last week? What about everything you told me?"

"I don't know," Nadia said again.

"What are you hiding?" Laurie said.

"Maybe it's just about sex," said Nadia. "Maybe that's all she really wanted from me."

"You really think that?" said Laurie. "Is the sex good?"

"It's amazing," Nadia said with enthusiasm. "Yeah... it's something. It's wild."

"Okay," said Laurie. "So maybe that's just fine for now. You're entitled to some fun."

"But I like her," said Nadia. "It's all just so strange, though. I don't know. Maybe it's lust talking. Maybe I'm blinded by her beauty, her position. All that."

"Nadia, you're all over the place," said Laurie. "I'm not really sure what's going on here."

"I'm sorry."

"What is it that you want?" Laurie asked empathetically. "What are you looking for?"

"I want love," said Nadia sadly. "I want to be in love and I want to feel that passion. With Avery, I get this feeling like I'm just a play-thing. It's just a fling while she's in town to take over our company. It'll end as soon as she's done with Color Wheel, and then it's back to New York."

"Hold up," said Laurie, lifting her palm. "What did you say?"

"What?" said Nadia. "What did I say?"

"What did Avery tell you?" Laurie said with a growing sense of urgency. "What did she say about Color Wheel?"

Nadia sighed, and she took another drink. Laurie had an impatient expression on her face, looking like she was about to burst.

"They're just going to take it all over," said Nadia. "They're going to take our clients and close us down. Start getting your resume together."

"That bitch!" said Laurie, smacking the table. "I can't believe this. But of course they are, you know? That's just how this shit works. It's infuriating."

"I'm sorry," said Nadia. "Look, I'm not supposed to say anything about this but I don't know if I really care. I'm just disappointed. Disappointed in it all."

"Well, at least you got laid," said Laurie. She took a long drink from her bloody mary as Nadia simply watched. "But we've just put so much work into this company. It's messed up that this is how it's going to end."

"Don't say anything to anyone else at the office, all right?" said Nadia.

"Why?" Laurie replied. "Aren't you pissed at Avery, too?"

"It's not that simple," said Nadia. "I really feel like something's there. But it's… complicated. I hate that word."

"I've got a friend," said Laurie quickly. "Mandy. She works for Digimedia in River North. I bet I could get us both interviews over there. We just need to jump ship while we still have jobs. It's much easier to get hired to a new job when you already have a job. If we get laid off, we could get screwed."

"Okay," acquiesced Nadia. "That's fine."

"*Whatever*, you know?" said Laurie, her anger obviously fomenting as she stewed longer on it. "These big companies don't give a damn about you. All they care about is money. And executives like Avery. They're all so rich and big, they couldn't care less about people like us. People who work so hard to build something, only for them to tear it down without a second thought."

"I think we both knew something like this was going to happen," said Nadia. "When Frances told us that Color Wheel had been bought out, we all protested and we said these exact fears. In a way, it's not really surprising at all."

"I guess I'm spending Sunday night with my laptop," said Laurie. "It's been a while since I updated my resume."

"Maybe we can do it together," said Nadia with a half-smile. Laurie's frown slowly turned into a smile like Nadia's and then she nodded affirmatively.

"Life goes on," said Laurie after another moment.

"You know, there's always the possibility we could transfer to New York and work at Scheffler & Vonn," Nadia posited. "I'm sure that's not out of the question."

"Do you want to move to New York?"

"Not really."

"Okay, then," said Laurie. "Resumes it is."

Laurie smiled more confidently this time and took another sip of her drink. Nadia didn't feel any better about her own situation. But the bloody mary helped dull it a little bit, at least.

Later on in the afternoon, Nadia was back in her condo straightening things up. She and Laurie had decided to meet at Nadia's place after dinner to work on updating their resumes together. It was late spring, the weather was warm, and a refreshing breeze came in through Nadia's open windows. As she fluffed the pillows on her couch in preparation for later, Nadia heard her phone begin to ring over in the kitchen. She stopped what she was doing and made her way over to answer it.

When she looked at the caller ID, she felt a chill. It was Avery.

"Hello?" said Nadia carefully when she answered.

"Nadia," said Avery. "How are you?"

"All right," said Nadia. "How are you?"

"I must admit," said Avery. "I'm really torn up about how things ended the other night. I wish you wouldn't have left."

"I guess I was just feeling betrayed," admitted Nadia. "I was really hurt and I just needed to go home."

"I completely understand that," said Avery. "And like I said to you, this isn't so black and white. You must understand my position."

"I do," said Nadia. "I get it. But it just makes me feel bad. Things were getting off to a good start with us, and then…"

"I have a proposition for you," said Avery plainly.

"Okay."

"Come on a business trip with me," Avery stated. "I have to go to New York at the end of this week for a meeting at corporate on Friday. I could certainly use one of our best account managers there with me."

"In the meeting?" Nadia asked with confusion. "You want me to attend the meeting with you?"

"Well, *no*," said Avery. "No, you wouldn't be coming to the meeting."

"So why should I go then?" said Nadia.

"For morale," said Avery. "For a free trip to New York. For a weekend getaway. Jesus, Nadia, come to New York with me, won't you please?"

Nadia was silent as she considered Avery's offer. Despite the growing complexity in their relationship, Nadia did have feelings for Avery. That was obvious to her, and something she couldn't deny. But how would Laurie feel about it? If Nadia continued on seeing Avery, would her best friend consider her to be sleeping with the enemy? It was a tough spot to be in.

"Can I tell you tomorrow?" asked Nadia. "At the office. I'm not sure I can make this decision right now."

"Of course," said Avery. "Yes, please do tell me tomorrow. I really hope you'll agree to come. I'll show you through the Scheffler & Vonn offices. I'll introduce you to some key people."

"I'll consider it," said Nadia. "I appreciate the offer. But I have to go now."

"All right," said Avery. "I look forward to your answer tomorrow, Nadia. And I hope you have a wonderful evening."

"Thank you," replied Nadia. "I'll see you then."

"Yes," said Avery. "Goodbye, Nadia."

"Goodbye, Avery."

Nadia hung up the phone and she sighed loudly and annoyedly. Slinking down into one of her barstool chairs at her counter, she held her head in her hands and wondered what the hell she was getting herself into.

WITH ONE LEG crossed over the other, Nadia sat in Frances' new office. Frances had cleared out of her former office to make way for Avery, and she had already moved a lot of things home. There was very little left and it looked like a temporary space. But Frances didn't seem to mind. She had her laptop set up and a stack of folders to the side of it. And ever since the acquisition had gone through, Frances appeared much more relaxed and much happier.

"So how can I help you, dear?" Frances asked Nadia. She adjusted her glasses and smiled warmly.

"I'm feeling a bit lost," Nadia admitted. "Ever since the buy-out and Avery, I'm feeling somewhat rudderless here at Color Wheel."

"Oh?" said Frances. "I think that's a common way to feel when things change."

"You don't appear to feel that way," said Nadia.

"Nadia, I worked very hard for a long time," said Frances. "And not to be crass about it, but I got my payout. I finally feel retired and it was a long time coming."

"I understand," said Nadia. She wrestled with what she knew. Frances must know as well, but she was playing dumb. She was pretending as though everything would keep on as it always had, and Nadia knew that to be untrue.

"I think you'll find Avery more than capable to run this business," Frances went on. "She has a tremendous pedigree. She has the power of a long-operating advertising company behind her. I see good things ahead for Color Wheel and for all of us."

"Frances," said Nadia with some exasperation in her voice. "I know what's going on."

"What's that supposed to mean?"

"It's come to my attention that the whole point of Scheffler & Vonn buying Color Wheel was to take our large clients," said Nadia. "The clients we've worked so hard to keep and maintain. They want the contracts, and once they have that they just plan to toss us aside."

"That's silly," said Frances with a laugh. "Whatever rumors are going around—"

"No, it's not rumors," said Nadia. "I know it's a fact. You don't have to pretend with me. I'm not going to tell anyone else what I know. But it just makes me feel... disappointed. Disappointed and lost and unmotivated."

Frances paused and her face grew serious. She straightened herself up in her chair and looked directly at Nadia. It took her a moment before she spoke, as she was mulling what she might possibly say over in her mind.

"They gave us a year," said Frances. "I wanted to make sure everybody here had a chance to make a move before they executed their plans. I made sure it was built in to the sale."

"I'm not so sure that it's going to hold up," said Nadia. "I think they have some other tricks up their sleeves to get what they want sooner than that."

"What makes you say that?" asked Frances.

"I just... it doesn't matter how I know," said Nadia. "But I think a lot of people here are going to feel the rug pulled out from underneath them. I don't expect it to take a year."

Frances paused again, once more deep in thought about the ideas coming from Nadia. She looked straight ahead in silence with seriousness in her face. But soon, that seriousness melted into acquiescence. Her face softened.

"Look," said Frances. "This is just business. I know you feel ownership over your clients, especially Polly, and that you've put in a lot of work. But a company like Scheffler & Vonn can't be stopped. Nadia, they've been around since the

50s. They represent some of the largest corporations in the world. They are a freight train of advertising prowess and it was either sell out to them, or risk having everything I worked for destroyed. Do you understand what I'm telling you?"

"I do."

"It was cheaper for them to buy us than to compete and run us out of business," said Frances. "And it was the best deal of my life. There was nothing else I could do."

"So what do we do?" asked Nadia. "What do *I* do?"

"First, you don't tell anyone else about this," said Frances. "That will cause a panic and it will only make things more difficult for everyone."

"I won't," Nadia agreed.

"Second, figure out where your life might take you next," Frances continued. "You're a talented woman and you will of course always get a sterling recommendation from me."

"So I should be thinking about a new job," said Nadia.

"I think that would probably be a good idea," said Frances.

"What are you going to do?" Nadia said. "Now that you're retiring and will never have to work again?"

"I just put an offer in on a home outside of Boulder, Colorado," said Frances, a pleased smile moving over her lips. "I hope to hike and ski and live a serene life with my husband and our dog."

"That's sounds pretty nice," said Nadia with an obvious tone of malaise.

"Nadia, you're going to be just fine," Frances reassured her. "This is not the end of the world. This is how things happen sometimes. And if you look at it from my perspective, it's the goal of being a business owner. You hope that one day all your hard work pays off and you can ride into the sunset."

"Right," said Nadia. "I get it."

"Why don't you try to get back to work?" asked Frances. "Your clients will appreciate your attentiveness to their accounts."

"Okay," said Nadia, pushing herself up out of the chair. "Thank you, Frances."

"You're welcome," Frances replied. "And please... don't tell anyone about this. Don't tell them what you've told me. You'll do more harm than good."

"I won't," said Nadia. She offered Frances a weak smile before turning from her and quickly exiting the office.

As Nadia sauntered down the hall, arms folded across her chest, she had a lot on her mind. Most of it entailed self-preservation. She didn't want to come into work one day to find out that her job was ending. She had to be ready for that, and she had to get out before things really started to get crazy. Laurie was right, and it was a good thing they had begun work on their resumes. She couldn't be sure where she landed next, but she hoped that she could continue working side-by-side with her best friend.

With so much on her mind, Nadia was oblivious to where she was in the office until she heard a very familiar voice call out to her.

"Nadia," said the voice. Nadia stopped, and she turned. She was in front of Avery's office. Avery smiled knowingly at her and leaned back against her desk.

Nadia just felt frozen there in the doorway. She found herself simultaneously adoring Avery and angered with her. The attraction was real, it was visceral, but the corporate interests that Avery represented made Nadia feel upset and powerless.

"Are you just going to stand there?" asked Avery. "Why don't you come in?"

Nadia followed instructions. She stepped inside of Avery's office and walked up to her.

"Hello," said Avery. She had a bright smile on her face.

"Hello."

"Well?" said Avery plainly. "May I have your answer?"

"My answer?" said Nadia.

"About the business trip," said Avery. "Are you going to come with me or not?"

"To New York?" said Nadia, immediately feeling silly about her clarification. Of course it was about New York. "Avery, I just don't know."

"What's your hesitation?" Avery questioned. "Why wouldn't you want to come with me? Don't you like me?"

Nadia paused and made a face like she was internally fighting with herself.

"Of course I like you," Nadia said after her moment of struggle. "I'm just upset about how this is happening. You don't expect a relationship to begin while you simultaneously lose everything else you know. You don't expect to gain a lover and lose a job at the same time."

"Nadia, darling," said Avery. "You don't seriously think you're going to truly lose your job, do you?"

"If Scheffler & Vonn steals all of our major clients, yeah, I do," said Nadia. "I don't expect we'll be needed if Color Wheel has no more clients."

Avery slowly stepped closer to Nadia, still smiling, still looking as though she were in control.

"Stick with me," said Avery. "You're not going to lose anything."

"What about everyone else here?" said Nadia. "What about my friends and coworkers?"

"I can only make this promise to you," Avery replied in a breathy whisper. "I can't save everyone. But you... you I can save."

Nadia felt her anger melting away. She couldn't help it. Avery made her feel wanted, lusted after, desired. Never did Nadia have such an experience. It did feel like some game, as Avery had presented to her. It was exciting, and that was something difficult to admit for Nadia.

"So why don't you come with me to New York?" Avery said once again. "I promise we'll have a good time."

Nadia was silent. But then a small smile came over her and she slowly nodded.

"Okay," said Nadia. "I'll come."

"You certainly will," said Avery. She grinned deeply. And Nadia could feel that grin pierce her, cut right to her heart, and intoxicate her with a passion she had never felt before.

THE SEATS in first class were large and cushy. There were only two seats on their side of the aisle, so Nadia and Avery had a private enclave within which they could speak candidly. When they sat down, the head stewardess brought them each a mimosa, an experience Nadia had never had before. She'd only flown coach in the past, and never had she been treated with such attentiveness on an airplane. The stewardess had returned multiple times before take-off to make sure the women were comfortable and had everything they needed.

Nadia and Avery had left work early on Thursday, as Avery's meeting was Friday at 8AM and she hated the red-eye flight. Avery was in good spirits as the trip kicked off, obviously happy that Nadia had joined her but she was also quite excited about the meeting. It sparked Nadia's interest.

"So what is this meeting about, anyhow?" Nadia asked, taking a sip of her mimosa.

"The board is meeting to discuss our acquisitions," Avery responded with a smile. "Such as Color Wheel, and a few other businesses we're invested in. As well as to discuss the shape of the board and the executive positions over the next few quarters. If you can't tell, I am excited about these propositions."

"I can tell," Nadia said with a sweet smile. "You've had a great attitude all day." Avery laughed.

"As though I don't normally have a great attitude," she quipped. "You're something."

"That's not what I meant," Nadia replied, laughing happily. "I just mean that you've been all smiles today."

"Well, I can share with you," Avery said, setting her glass down on the seat-back tray in front of her. "I've already told you so much, why not spill the rest?"

"Is this something that might throw me into crisis?" said Nadia. She slowly grinned.

"Oh, don't be silly," countered Avery. "It's about me."

"Okay, I'm listening."

"Indeed," said Avery, obviously getting excited. "The CEO of Scheffler & Vonn, John Lockheed, is... how do I put this politely? He's getting up there in years."

"He's old," said Nadia.

"That's putting it lightly," Avery said, laughing a tickled laugh. "He's not long for this world, as dreary an image as that is. And talk of his retirement has been going around for years. Well, about a year ago I spoke with his son, Harris Lockheed, who is a member of the board, and he indicated that his father was seriously considering retirement."

"All right," said Nadia, smiling, and giving a nod. "So?"

"So," repeated Avery. "I left my position to take over as CEO at Color Wheel, packed up my life and moved to Chicago, to show my leadership capabilities. I am vying for that position, Nadia. They all know it. I am hoping that the plan come John's retirement is to name me CEO of Scheffler & Vonn." Avery smiled wide.

"You think that this meeting will be to name you future CEO of the company?" asked Nadia.

"Now, I don't know that for *sure*," corrected Avery. "But I feel it. I'm a perfect fit. They want greater diversity in the company, and naming a female CEO would be enormous for optics. Nadia, let's be real. Scheffler & Vonn has an absolutely *dire* reputation for being an old school advertising firm. They know they need to change that. And as far as that current board goes, I'm their only hope."

"How can you work for a company like that?" Nadia asked, unable to mask her distaste. "A company that would make you CEO just to look good in the eyes of the public?"

"Nadia," said Avery plainly. "That's how *all* companies work. It's all about how things look, you see. The public is very myopic in that regard. That's simply the way of the world."

"And you're fine with that?"

"I want to be CEO," Avery said and smiled. "I'll take what I can get. And," she continued, giving Nadia a gentle nudge. "It's good to be in with the CEO."

Nadia smiled flatly and eased back into her seat. After a moment of silence, she picked up her glass and took another drink.

"You're a worrier, aren't you?" Avery said after a beat. She lifted her eyebrows as Nadia turned her head and looked at her.

"Sometimes," said Nadia.

"What has worrying ever got you?" continued Avery. "You know it only makes you suffer twice if those worries come true."

"Explain that," Nadia replied.

"If you worry about something and it never comes to

pass, you tore yourself up over nothing," Avery said. "If you worry about something and it does indeed happen as you feared, you not only suffered when you were worrying, but you also must suffer now. It's a pointless exercise."

"But it pays to prepare, doesn't it?" asked Nadia. "Worrying can help you mentally prepare for the worst."

"To a point, sure," said Avery. "But I bet you dwell. I but you lie awake at night sometimes worrying about things completely out of your control."

"Doesn't everyone?" Nadia said incredulously.

"They don't," Avery said. She smiled. "I don't."

"It's easy not to worry when you're rich," Nadia countered. Avery laughed.

"I suppose that helps," said Avery. "But money doesn't solve all problems. And sometimes, it can even be the *cause* of problems."

"My worry is that my job will be going away," said Nadia. "That's out of my control, but it still affects me. I have bills to pay. And I worked so hard to get where I am."

"I told you not to worry about that," Avery said. "And even if you didn't have me in your corner, you are not someone who has to worry about finding another job. You are smart and dedicated and beautiful. You will be just fine."

"You're so flippant sometimes," huffed Nadia, crossing her arms. "I'm beginning to hate how much I like you." This gave Avery an even bigger laugh than before.

"What do you like about me?" Avery asked with a wide smile on her face. "Stroke my ego, please."

"Your confidence," said Nadia. "I wish I could have more of that."

"It's a gift," Avery said.

"Your charisma," Nadia went on. "Despite the fact that you're responsible for the coming end of my job, I can't help myself but like being with you."

"Now hold on," said Avery, holding up a finger. "I am not responsible for what's happening with Color Wheel. I am simply responsible for enacting the chain of events that will fulfill the corporate plan."

"It's the same thing," said Nadia.

"It's really not," said Avery. "This is just business, anyway. This kind of thing happens every day. You're not naive to that."

"I am not," agreed Nadia.

"All of that can exist," said Avery with the wave of a hand. "Alongside *this*," she said, motioning between her and Nadia.

"And what is this?" Nadia asked. "What exactly is going on here?"

"Do you like what's going on between us?" Avery said.

"Yes," said Nadia.

"I do, too," Avery replied and smiled. "Let's just see where it all leads. The journey is my favorite part."

"Another thing I like about you," Nadia said. "Is that you're so cagey. It riles me up, because it can be so infuriating, but it can also be so incredibly alluring. It's madness."

"You know, at first I was just physically attracted to you," said Avery. "Then it was your mind. And now, I think, what

I enjoy most about you is that you're not afraid to call me out."

Nadia smirked and then found herself laughing along with Avery.

"I think you have plenty of confidence," Avery continued. Reaching over, she took Nadia's hand and held to it tightly. "You just need the proper inspiration to let it out."

"Maybe that's right," said Nadia. She smiled, looking down at their joined hands. This whole relationship had come as a huge surprise to Nadia. It still didn't make complete sense. But she was happy where she found herself, sitting next to Avery in first class, flying out to New York City, on her way to one of the most well-known ad agencies in the country. It was a whirlwind, and Nadia was enjoying it for all its ups and downs.

She tried to take Avery's advice, and reassured herself that she had no need to worry. Nadia needn't look any further than where she currently was. Her life was really beginning to get exciting.

WHEN AVERY OPENED the door to her condo, Nadia's eyes widened. It was probably the nicest and most well-curated living space she had ever seen in her life. Much more than Avery's rental in Chicago, this space looked as though it were straight out of a magazine. It was white and clean and modern, with an entire wall of windows that faced out toward Central Park. An open layout, the kitchen boasted professional stainless steel equipment, a quartz countertop island, and a centralized view of the fantastically appointed living room. It was obvious this space had cost its owner a lot of money.

"Wow," Nadia said, stepping inside and looking around. "This is where you live?"

"It's not much, but it's home," joked Avery. She grinned.

The women wheeled their suitcases off to the side of the foyer, while Nadia couldn't take her eyes off of the condo. Everything was immaculate. The sun was beginning to set and a magical light shone in through the floor to ceiling windows.

"This place makes your condo in Chicago look like a hotel room," remarked Nadia.

"My rental in Chicago essentially *is* a hotel room," said Avery. She waltzed into the kitchen, opened the refrigerator, and plucked out a bottle of white wine. As Avery opened the bottle and prepared the glasses, Nadia stepped further into the living room and looked out of the window. The view of Central Park was just like a picture. She couldn't believe she was experiencing it from this vantage. It made her feel special.

"I can't imagine what you think about my loft," Nadia mused.

"I like your loft," said Avery with a smile, stepping closer to Nadia and handing her a glass. Nadia took it and drank. "It has so many rustic qualities, it feels very warm."

"Did you design this place yourself?" Nadia asked. "It's just... it's so curated."

"If only I had those abilities," said Avery with a small laugh. "No, I paid a designer quite handsomely for this work."

"It certainly shows," said Nadia.

"I do regret not having a balcony," Avery said. "But this building has no outdoor space. Apart from the penthouse, which is owned by someone quite famous." She smiled devilishly and drank.

"Are you not going to tell me who it is?" said Nadia impatiently.

"I really shouldn't," said Avery. "I try to respect their privacy, you understand."

"You're playing with me, aren't you?" Nadia said, mimicking Avery's grin.

"I might be."

"Well, I don't care to know," replied Nadia. "It doesn't bother me at all."

"Not that he's your type," Avery began. "But he's a ruggedly handsome gentleman who has starred in many major blockbuster films. Though he got his start on a medical drama in the 90s."

"George—"

"Ah ah," Avery said, holding up a finger. "Let's respect his privacy."

"I imagine this building is filled with people like him," said Nadia. "Is there anybody who has a condo here that might be a bit more... *interesting* to me?"

"Hmm," intoned Avery, taking another drink and thinking about Nadia's question. "There's a very busty young starlet who owns a place in the building that you might enjoy. In fact, her first name rhymes with *starlet*."

"Oh yes," Nadia said with a laugh. "Yes, I know exactly who you mean. She's a hot one, definitely."

"And she's feisty," said Avery. "I've hit on her before in the elevator, and she was quite receptive. She played along, but I imagine she's way out of my league. And I don't believe she's gay, so there's that also."

"She's not out of your league," countered Nadia. "Are you kidding? You're stunning."

"That's very nice of you to say," said Avery. She leaned in and placed a gentle kiss on Nadia's lips. "Besides, I don't need *Starlet* now, do I?"

"No," said Nadia. She returned Avery's kiss and the two of them began tenderly kissing one another, each holding their wine glass up in the air so as not to spill. The kissing continued and Nadia could feel her heart swell and she could feel the excitement growing inside of her.

"Do you know what I like after a flight?" Avery asked seductively between kisses.

"What's that?" replied Nadia in a quiet but eager tone.

"I like a nice shower," said Avery. "Flying makes me feel a bit dirty."

"A shower sounds nice," said Nadia.

"Care to join me?"

"Yes," said Nadia. She stepped back from their kiss, she smiled, and then Nadia took a large gulp of her wine. Avery followed suit, quickly finishing her drink. The two of them grinned enthusiastically at one another in pregnant silence.

Water rained down on Nadia's back. She was sitting on her knees, perched on the tiled floor of the large shower. The bathroom was well-lit with soft light, yet the shower had a certain dimness to it thanks to the dark tile of the shower stall. They were enclosed in glass that had begun to fog from the humidity of the water. Avery leaned back against the wall, her limber body stretched, trickles of water running down her flesh. Nadia's hands wrapped around Avery, gripping to her ass, while she buried her face into Avery's pussy, licking and sucking with intense adoration.

Nadia revered in pleasuring Avery. It aroused her to no end, and as she ate out her boss there in the shower, she could feel herself growing hot and wet, eager to be touched and pleasured in kind. Her heart throbbed for Avery, and the more intimate their relationship grew, the more Nadia felt like this was something real, something special. Looking up the length of Avery's body, still keeping her lips pressed to Avery's wet lips, Nadia could see the look of passion plastered all over Avery's face.

"That's so good," moaned Avery, delicately playing with Nadia's shower-damp hair. Avery looked down, and she caught eyes with Nadia. She smiled admiringly. Nadia refocused, she wrapped her lips around Avery's clit, and she sucked deeply. Avery shuddered.

Never had Nadia had such a whirlwind relationship, and never had she had sex as hot as the sex she had with Avery. It made her feel as though she'd missed out in the past, yet she was thrilled with the excitement that the present had to offer. Thoughts of all of her exes had ceased to occupy her brain. Even the thoughts and worries of her career seemed to dissipate when she was being intimate with Avery. It felt, in these moments of passion, that she was truly living.

At one point, Avery turned herself around so that her back faced Nadia. She bent over, leaned into the wall, and presented her backside. Without even thinking about it, Nadia pushed her face between Avery's ass cheeks and she licked from behind. Water ran down her face as she kissed her lover's ass, and bringing a hand up, she pushed two fingers up inside of Avery. Avery's arousal made the penetration easy and the groans coming from up above let Nadia know she was on the right track.

Soon enough, Nadia herself was standing and leaning firmly back against the wall while Avery stood in front of her, pressing into her, the two women heatedly and wildly making out. Avery held a small vibrating toy, and she had it pressed against Nadia's clit. Her other hand groped at Nadia's chest, squeezing her aching breasts with urgency and lust.

The loving attention, the kissing, the groping, and the vibration of the toy on her hot button was making Nadia sweat. She was becoming so pent up with excited energy, Nadia felt as though she was going to burst. Leaning her head against the wall behind her, Nadia moaned out and this admittance of pleasure only made Avery work harder.

Avery squeezed onto Nadia's tit and then Nadia felt the vibrations begin. It wasn't much longer before her limbs were buzzing and she was shaking. A few expletives left her mouth, and when it was obvious that she was having an orgasm, Avery only took it further. She held the pulsating toy against Nadia with her palm, while she deftly pushed back and forth between Nadia's pussy lips with the same hand. Nadia couldn't stop her moaning. Each breath brought with it a cry of ecstasy. She was coming hard, and Avery was not going to let it stop.

Once Nadia was completely spent, she stumbled, braced herself on the wall, and Avery caught her. The women looked each other in the eye and they laughed. Nadia's face looked exasperated, she was panting, she was smiling, she looked like she needed a rest. Avery kissed her once slowly and tenderly.

"That was amazing," said Nadia as soon as the ability to form words came back to her. "Holy shit, I don't think I've ever come that hard before."

"This little devil is something else," said Avery, holding up the purple, vibrating toy. She flicked at it and it ceased in its frenzy.

"Oh my God," said Nadia, putting a hand to her own forehead, still trying to catch her breath. "You're so good at that."

"I've got about ten years experience on you," teased Avery. "But I could teach you a couple of things if you like. Think of it as a shortcut from an old professional."

"Wow," Nadia mused, still holding her head. She was reeling from her orgasm, her body exhausted in post-coital bliss. Her eyes darted to Avery, who was smiling back at her. Nadia smiled in return and, in that moment, with water still streaming down in the shower, she felt real unbridled happiness. It was a feeling she could easily get used to.

———————

THE WALLS in the conference room at the Scheffler & Vonn offices were oak and they were impeccably maintained. The table in the middle of the room, a matching color and finish to the walls, was long and thick and large. It looked as though it could never be moved. Around the table were a slew of executives, every one of them dressed in tailored suits of the finest material. This was a billion dollar company, after all, and the board reflected that kind of wealth.

John Lockheed, the CEO of the company, sat at the head of the table. He looked disaffected, worn out, and old. He had been sitting around this table for much of his life and had known both Marc Scheffler and William Vonn on a personal level. Other executives, based on their seniority and power, lined the sides of the table. This included John's son Harris, as well as Martin Shaw, the chief operating officer and Avery's direct boss. Avery sat further down the table than she was used to, as her role had changed. Her old seat was now occupied by Paul Wheeler, the new chief administrating officer that had replaced Avery when she left for Chicago.

The room was stuffy. Not just for the lack of circulating air, but also because of the people in it. It didn't feel like a very progressive or forward-thinking bunch.

"I do think we need to look to these emerging markets for new opportunities," said Harris Lockheed. He had been with the company for over thirty years, and he looked a lot like his father. It was a look of old money. "Especially as household wages increase and people find themselves with more buying power."

"Paul, I want you to put your team on looking into China in particular," said Martin. "If there's a McDonald's in Hong Kong, we can certainly get our fast-food clients in as well."

"Certainly," said Paul, scribbling something down in his notes.

"I think we're on the right track," said Harris. "Next, let's discuss some of our more recent acquisitions. Martin?"

"Yes," said Martin. "Specifically we've purchased a handful of smaller agencies that have been making waves with corporate clients across the country. The plan has been to absorb these agencies, pluck the large clients away, and liquidate the companies once we have the clients. One of the most notable in this is an agency in Chicago called Color Wheel. They won the contract for Polly smartphones, beating us out as well as a few other large firms. However, we've purchased this company and are now in the process of completing the plan. Avery, do you have anything to add?"

"Right," said Avery. "I've taken over as CEO of Color Wheel and have taken stock of their client roster. They indeed have multiple large corporate clients that we would be interested in, Polly most of all. Stipulated in the purchase contract, we cannot make any major moves with clients or employees until a year after we took ownership. However, legally speaking, we could move many of these accounts to New York, setup a Color Wheel office in name only, and begin the process of transitioning these clients over to us."

"This has been the plan all along," Martin said, moving his attention from Avery back up to John and Harris. "We appeased the owner of the company with a clause we knew we could get around."

"It's not clear to me," said Avery, eying Martin and then Paul and then back to Martin. "What will become of my role once the transition is complete. I gave up my old position to take this on, and I want to be assured that I will have a place."

"We'll certainly address that at a later date," said Martin. But Avery was a very sharp woman. There was something in his voice and in his face that worried her. It felt as though he were brushing her off.

"With all due respect," said Avery. "I accepted this role to prove my dedication to Scheffler & Vonn. I'm hoping that the board sees that I have much more to offer this organization."

"I'm not sure this conversation is very constructive at this point," interjected Harris. "Let's continue with the plan of absorbing the clients of this agency, as well as the others, as Martin sees fit."

Avery bit her tongue. There wasn't much else she could do.

The meeting continued on in a similar fashion, each executive having a turn to speak about their current projects and bring up any issues they faced. Avery tried to pay attention, but her mind was fixated. She couldn't help but worry about how Martin had spoke, how he had looked, and the way Harris blew her off. It made her angry, but at this point she was powerless to do anything. In these kind of situations, she had learned, it was best not to rock the boat, as crushing as that realization could be.

"And finally," said Martin. "I believe we have one final issue to address." He had a smile on his face as he looked to the head of the table. "John, the floor is all yours."

"Thank you, Martin," John said in a gruff, low voice. "After working with Scheffler & Vonn for over sixty years, this wonderful company that gave me my very first job, and serving as its CEO now for twenty years, my time has come to step down and retire so that I might spend my golden years with my family."

A very demure applause resounded through the room.

"Yes," John continued. "While it's up to the board to determine who takes over after I make my exit, I'd like to nominate my son, Harris Lockheed, to ascend to this role. We are a meritocracy here at Scheffler & Vonn, and very few have been more dedicated to the company than Harris. It was very important to the founders of this company that it remain in the family, and I needn't remind any of you that William Vonn's granddaughter Colleen is Harris' wife. I think you'll all find giving Harris the reins will be a move that will secure this company's future."

There was a positive response from the board, many people nodding in agreement or voicing their consent.

Harris smiled and looked down at the table. But Avery was unmoved by John Lockheed's speech. Her facial expression didn't show it, but the anger she felt had now doubled. Surely she could agree that Harris had done more time in the company than most anybody else, but his ideas were the same as his father's. It was old thinking, it was a thing of the past, and Avery knew that she could lead Scheffler & Vonn into the future. But now, that would never be.

And in fact, her entire position at the firm was up in the air. Avery didn't know what to think anymore.

After the meeting had ended and the board dispersed, Avery chased down Martin in the hallway, walking by his side as he tried to rush away from the conference room. When he looked to Avery, he had a busy expression on his face, but it had a falseness to it.

"Martin," said Avery. "Can I speak with you for a moment?"

"I really need to get back to my office," said Martin. "Can we chat on the phone next week?"

"It'll only take a minute," asserted Avery. Martin took a breath and he stopped.

"Okay," he said. "What can I do for you?"

"I must know what my position will be with Scheffler & Vonn once we shut Color Wheel down," said Avery. "Paul's placement in my old job does not seem temporary, and I will not stand for silence on this matter. I deserve to know."

Martin crossed his arms and looked at Avery in silence for a moment. Then his face softened.

"I know you don't like bullshit, Avery," he said. "So I will spare you."

"Please do."

"The board is pushing you out," said Martin. "They're unimpressed with your ideas, many of which would necessitate painful change on this organization. Harris will obviously take over once John retires, and that means more of the same. They're not ready for what you're trying to tell them."

"But Martin," protested Avery. "I took this transfer specifically—"

"I know you did," Martin interrupted. "But it was seen as a convenient move for many on the board. I'm sorry, Avery. Once you're finished in Chicago, when you come back here you will be given a lower-level management position in administration. You will not return to your executive position."

"I was hired on as an executive," said Avery. "You're telling me that I will be demoted?"

"I'm sorry, Avery," said Martin. "This is the way it will be."

"I understand," Avery replied, maintaining her composure. "Thank you for being straight with me, Martin."

"I appreciate your understanding," said Martin. "And I know this won't affect the work you do in Chicago."

"It certainly will not," said Avery.

"This is just business," Martin continued on. "Don't take it personally. You know how this company is. They've been doing things for a certain way for a very long time, and they are not keen to change what has worked for them. When I came on here, I was just as surprised as you are but we will not be changing anything around here in the near term."

"Thank you," said Avery. "I will return to Chicago and be in touch about the progress."

"Thank you, Avery," said Martin. "And again, I'm sorry."

He offered her a flat smile and then, after a moment of silence, he walked off from Avery. She watched him leave and felt a fire igniting deep inside of her. Martin was right. Scheffler & Vonn was an old company with old ideas. But she really thought she would be the one to change that. She knew that even Martin himself was on board. Harris and some of the others, however, were not. And now all Avery could do was accept her fate and figure out what came next.

NADIA STOOD in the kitchen of Avery's condo, leaning on the island, holding a glass of water with both hands. She watched as Avery stared out of the window in the living room, gazing down on Central Park below. Avery was silent, ruminating, and ever since her meeting the day before, she hadn't been the same Avery that Nadia had come to know. There was something going on inside of her and Nadia felt the urge to help. However, it was a sensitive topic that she wasn't sure how to broach.

Standing up straight, Nadia made her way toward Avery with careful and deliberate steps. She didn't want to sneak up on her. As she closed in, Avery turned her head and caught eyes with Nadia. Avery smiled weakly, and then returned her gaze to the outdoors.

"It's going to be okay," said Nadia gingerly. She raised her hand and delicately rubbed Avery's shoulder blade.

"Yes," said Avery with a slow nod. "I know."

"Do you want to talk about it?" Nadia asked. She offered a small smile as Avery looked to her once more.

"This certainly isn't the trajectory I wanted to take," Avery replied. "I really believed things were on the rise for me at the company. But this was a trick."

"I'm sure you can see the irony in that," said Nadia. Avery nodded.

"Of course," she said. "It's not lost on me."

"Taking a page out of your book," Nadia said. "Maybe we should resolve to not worry. Right? I mean, this is happening, and we have to accept it. But you're fine. It's not like this is dire straits for you. You aren't going broke, and you'll be able to find a new job elsewhere."

"I just put a lot of hope into this," said Avery. "I thought things were changing at Scheffler & Vonn. But it's still an old boys club. What a fool I was."

"No," said Nadia empathetically. "You're not a fool at all. Of course Scheffler & Vonn is like this. Of course the CEO would pass the position off to his son. That's not your fault. I've been disappointed ever since I found out what was happening with Color Wheel, it's been really sad for me. But it's not a surprise."

"You left my condo when you found out," countered Avery.

"I was overcome with emotion," said Nadia. "In a way, I had already known what was happening. I just couldn't admit it. I knew ever since Frances announced the buy-out to us months ago. When you made it real, I just felt like I was falling. I should have stayed."

"You don't hate me, Nadia, do you?" asked Avery tenderly. "Being a powerful, emotionless businesswoman is taxing. But the truth is, I do have emotions. I just simply must suppress them if I want to succeed."

"I don't hate you," Nadia said, a smile moving over her lips. "The opposite. I know I haven't known you very long, but I really enjoy being with you. I'm in awe of you, really."

"In awe," Avery scoffed with a laugh. "That's very sweet of you, but I really don't deserve it."

"But it's true," replied Nadia. "You're so successful and skilled. Everybody looks up to you. You command respect in the office, and I think that's simultaneously inspiring and scary." Avery laughed and she looked on at Nadia with doting eyes.

"Scary, eh?" said Avery. "I suppose I can be somewhat imposing."

"I think those of us with bigger dreams look at you with envy," said Nadia. "We want to know how to get into your position. We want to learn to be more like you."

Avery smiled and she looked away.

"What do you think is next?" Nadia asked softly.

"I can't rightfully stay at Scheffler & Vonn," said Avery. "I won't accept a demotion from my executive position."

"But you're going to continue with the plan to close Color Wheel?" Nadia said.

"I don't know," said Avery. "It is my charge to do so, but I'm really not confident how I should proceed."

"What about your family business?" Nadia proposed. "Isn't that something you could go back to?"

"And give my father the satisfaction?" said Avery skeptically. "No, I don't believe that is something I could rightfully do." This was the first Nadia had heard of a possible rift in Avery's family, and it piqued her interest.

"What happened with your father?" said Nadia.

Avery turned from the window and she made her way toward the kitchen. Watching her for a moment, Nadia suddenly felt as though she might have said the wrong thing. Once Avery opened up a bottle of wine, Nadia followed her and walked up to the kitchen island, accepting the glass that Avery pushed her way.

"My father and I don't always see eye to eye," said Avery finally. She drank from her glass. "He can be quite demanding."

"Is that why you left the company?"

"You might say that," replied Avery. She paused and thought, trying to gather her words. "It was one of myriad reasons."

"You can be open with me," Nadia said, offering a reassuring smile. "I don't bite." Avery grinned, but there was still sadness in her expression.

"It's the same thing as what's happening with Scheffler & Vonn," said Avery with finality. "M. M. Wool Properties will be run by my brother when my father retires. Not me. I would be destined to play second fiddle were I to return. Surely, my father would love to have me back. It is our family business, after all. But he remains unmoved concerning my desire to be the CEO and president. And so, I had to break out on my own."

"It's a sexist world," mused Nadia. She took a drink.

"I loathe it," Avery said.

"I do, too."

"I really look up to Frances," said Avery. "After getting to know her and to see what she's built, I have a lot of respect for her."

"Agreed," said Nadia. "Frances is amazing."

"And then we came in and ruined it," Avery said, now with a sense of lament. She sighed and swirled her wine in the glass.

"I think Frances is pretty happy about it, ultimately," said Nadia. "She doesn't have to work ever again if she doesn't want to."

"Well, neither do I," said Avery.

"But you won't stop," Nadia said. "You're chasing something bigger."

"I've got a lot of years left," Avery said. "I won't be giving up any time soon."

"Listen," said Nadia, taking a drink for courage. "I don't imagine we can stop what Scheffler & Vonn will be doing with Color Wheel. It's only a matter of time before it's over.

A year at the most. Both Laurie and I have already been preparing our resumes and putting our feelers out."

"Laurie knows about this?" Avery asked sharply.

"I'm sorry," said Nadia. "She's my best friend, and my confidant. I had to tell her." Avery's sharpness faded quickly.

"Yes," said Avery, waving it off. "I suppose it doesn't matter."

"If Color Wheel is going down," continued Nadia. "And your position with Scheffler & Vonn is going down with it, maybe we can do something else. Something together."

Avery's ears perked up and she stood up straighter. She took a drink and her face looked thoughtful and accepting.

"What did you have in mind?" Avery asked after a moment.

"I..." Nadia started, but then she stopped herself. "I don't know. But, that doesn't matter right now. What does matter is that we don't let these things that our outside of our control rule us. We should do our own thing and run it how we like. I'm tired of working hard for a company only to have it snatched out from under me. There's just no security in working for someone else. If you want security, you've got to create your own."

"You're a smart one," said Avery, a reassured smile appearing on her face. She raised her glass up and Nadia did the same. They both drank.

Nadia felt very self-satisfied with her proposal, and Avery's receptiveness to it made it all the better. The fact that she had no specific plan didn't deter her at all. At least she knew that there was a path, even if that path was obscured. She knew that no matter what it was they decided to do, she would put in the effort required to make it happen. That was her strength. Nadia had worked her way up in Color Wheel, and in her career, and just like Avery, she was not about to take a step backwards.

"Thank you, Nadia," Avery said. "I'm very happy you and I were able to find each other. Quite a surprise, really. I never expected a relationship to flourish out of my transfer to Chicago."

"You thought it was just going to be some hot sex and then you'd run off back to New York?" teased Nadia with a devilish grin. Avery laughed.

"Perhaps that," Avery admitted. "But life has a way of giving you the things you need, precisely when you need them. Amid the chaos, there is hope."

"I like you, too," Nadia said happily. The women smiled at one another. There *was* hope. And it felt reassuring to know it was waiting for them.

ABOUT A MONTH LATER, the morale at Color Wheel had begun to tank. Frances had made her exit just as some of the bigger clients on their roster were being moved to the newly created New York office, staffed with employees from Scheffler & Vonn. There was growing talk of layoffs in Chicago, though nothing concrete had been announced. The overall attitude was grim, and a lot of negativity was being directed at Avery. She represented the end of an era for a once thriving business, and Color Wheel's staff was increasingly angered by her presence.

Avery's own attitude was wavering as well. She had come to hate her charge of dismantling the company, yet she maintained her authority when in the office, always acting like the boss that she was. It was all she could do. Avery and Nadia had spent many nights together, brain-storming the possibilities for a joint venture, but they had yet to come up with a viable plan. They weren't without hope, though the difficulties they faced appeared to be mounting.

Nadia sat in her office tapping into her keyboard, composing a message to her counterpart in New York who had taken over some of the duties in managing the Polly account. She knew that she was essentially training her replacement, all while making it seem to the client as though the company had simply grown. Nadia kept a positive atti-tude, though, because she could see the light at the end of the tunnel. It was just currently a bit blurry.

Suddenly Laurie burst in to her office, and she swiftly closed the door behind her. She grinned big at Nadia and leapt over toward her desk. Laurie sat down, still smiling.

"You look happy," teased Nadia.

"Oh, I am," said Laurie.

"What's going on?" asked Nadia, pushing her keyboard away and giving her friend her full attention.

"I got an interview," Laurie said. "With Digimedia. My friend Mandy came through. I'm pretty excited."

"That's awesome," said Nadia, smiling along with Laurie. "I'm happy for you."

"You could still apply," said Laurie. "I told Mandy what's happening over here and she said they're definitely looking for more people like us."

"I told you already," said Nadia. "I'm putting something together with Avery."

"Anything new with that?" replied Laurie.

"No."

"Give me your resume," said Laurie. "I'll send it to Mandy."

"I know it's crazy," said Nadia. "And I know that Avery's sort of the enemy around here, but things between us are going really well and I trust her. She's not on board with Scheffler & Vonn's plans anymore, but she's got to fulfill her duties."

"Does she?" countered Laurie. "She could always just quit."

"If she quits she'll have to go back to New York," said Nadia. "And she's got nothing else lined up."

"Doesn't she have the money to do whatever she wants?" Laurie asked. "She could probably just go on vacation for the next couple years and not even worry about it."

"Yeah, but that's not who she is," Nadia said. "I think she very much likes to feel useful and needed."

"Well, the writing is on the wall around here," said Laurie. "This place is a sinking ship and it's time to jump off. How are you doing with your work?"

"It's hard to stay focused, you know?" said Nadia. "I'm just sending a lot of my work to my New York counterpart, this woman Stacy. I spend a lot of time brainstorming business ideas to see if I can come up with something for Avery and I to work on." Nadia held up a notepad and gave a half-smile.

"I was really pissed off at first," said Laurie. "About all this. But I think it's an opportunity to grow. It's really given me a new insight on the way these type of companies operate. No loyalty to the employees. If that's the way they play it, that's the way *you've* got to play it."

"I just hope you don't hold a grudge against Avery," said Nadia. "She's experiencing the same thing we are. Her days are numbered as well."

"I know," Laurie said. She smiled. "I don't hold a grudge."

"Good," replied Nadia. "She really is a good person. This whole thing has just been a mess."

"Well," said Laurie, pushing herself up out of the chair and preparing to leave. "Just keep what I said in mind. I can get you in over at Digimedia. It's all up to you."

"I definitely appreciate that," said Nadia with a smile. "You're my best friend, Laurie."

"And you're mine," Laurie said. "Keep your chin up."

"Yes, ma'am," said Nadia. Laurie grinned at her and then exited Nadia's office. Nadia watched her go and she sighed, wondering if she should just give Laurie her resume and make the leap over to a new advertising agency.

A little later in the day, Nadia made her way down the hall and toward Avery's office. As she approached the door, she looked in and saw that Avery was on the telephone. Her voice was docile as she spoke, talking in a way that Nadia hadn't yet heard from her. Nadia couldn't help but try to listen in, and as soon as Avery saw her waiting, she waved for her to come in.

"Yes, of course," said Avery into the phone. She watched as Nadia sat in a chair across from her desk. "If you'd like my help, I will do whatever you need."

Nadia watched and listened. It was a different side of Avery than she was used to. It was very interesting.

"I look forward to seeing you, too," Avery went on. "Will Max be coming as well? Yes? That's terrific." Avery looked to Nadia and mouthed the words 'one minute.'

Nadia smiled and nodded.

"Splendid," said Avery. "We'll be in touch, then. Yes, I love you, too. Goodbye, Dad."

That's when Nadia's eyes lit up. Avery hung up her phone and she took a deep breath, letting it out in a long exhale.

"That was your father," Nadia said after a moment.

"It surely was," affirmed Avery.

"And he's coming here?" asked Nadia. "To Chicago?"

"Yes," said Avery. "Along with my brother Max and some of the other executives from the company. They're in the beginning stages of buying a building here in Chicago."

"Wow," said Nadia. "That's pretty exciting."

"He wants my help with a few things concerning the proposed building management contract," said Avery. "It's something I used to do when I worked for him. The woman who usually does it since I left is on maternity leave."

"And you're going to help him?"

"Yes, of course," said Avery. "He's family. And I'm still connected to the business."

"Will I get to meet them?" asked Nadia. "Your father and brother?"

Avery paused for a moment and she looked off. Nadia could tell she was thinking.

"You want to meet them?" she said finally, lifting a brow inquisitively. Nadia nodded quickly.

"Definitely," said Nadia. "I think meeting them will give me the deep insight I'm looking for to really figure you out." She grinned, and Avery laughed.

"All right," said Avery. "We'll do lunch while they're in town."

"And how will you introduce me?" teased Nadia. "This is my employee, Nadia Marek. She's very sharp!" Nadia laughed at herself, while Avery smiled and shook her head.

"You're cute," said Avery. "How should I introduce you?"

"As your girlfriend," said Nadia. "I mean, that's what I am, right?"

"Right," Avery replied. Her growing smile was warm and affectionate. "That's what you are."

Nadia beamed. She could feel her heart throb with excitement. Avery's complexity was beginning to melt away as Nadia got a better sense of her and their relationship. It only made Nadia feel more attracted to her.

"With that being said," Avery continued. "Are my girlfriend and I still on for this evening?"

"Yes, I do believe so," said Nadia. "Should I plan to stay over tonight?"

"I would think so," said Avery. She paused for a moment. "Have you come up with any new potential business ideas since we last spoke about it?"

"No," said Nadia. "I'm still thinking."

"Neither have I," conferred Avery. "It's much harder to start something from scratch than it is to join a business already in progress."

"We'll come up with something," Nadia said, a smile returning to her face. "I'm not too worried."

"I'm glad," said Avery. "I don't think women like us have much to worry about. We've got a lot of talent between us. And I'm glad that we're joining forces. Now, if only we had an idea." Nadia laughed.

"Maybe it'll come to us in bed," teased Nadia.

"Oh, I like that," said Avery. "Then we should spend more time in bed in the coming weeks. What do you say to that?"

"I'm on board," said Nadia. "Let's start tonight."

"Let's," said Avery. The women both grinned. They were thinking the very same thing.

NADIA WAS SITTING on the couch in her living room, leaning forward and looking into her open laptop on the coffee table. She had already left work for the day, but she was still working as her client Polly was out in California and a few time zones behind her. Summer sunlight shone in through her window, and Nadia was eager to get out and enjoy the mild evening before the sun started to go down. She held her phone to her ear with her shoulder as her fingers tapped on the keyboard.

"Yeah, Harold," she said into the phone. "It looks as though Stacy will be taking over that as well."

"What's going on over there?" Harold asked. "We've been working with you less and less, while it seems like the New York office is taking care of most of the work."

"Yeah, that's true," said Nadia. "I think they're trying for a successful launch of the New York office, and they're putting us on newer clients," she lied. "But I don't really make any of those higher level decisions."

"It just seems like there's a big shakeup," said Harold. "Are you doing okay?"

"I'm all right."

"Listen," said Harold. "I know you're happy living in Chicago, but if you ever feel the urge to come to sunny California, let me know. I might be able to figure out a spot for you here with us."

"Work directly for Polly?" said Nadia, sitting up straight and taking hold of her phone. "That's interesting."

"We've been really happy working with you, Nadia," he said. "And I don't really like what's going on here, if I'm being honest. Maybe we could poach you away and work something out."

"Let me think about that," said Nadia. "I never thought about moving to California. Well, I did for a moment," she said, suddenly remembering her ex. "But... who knows."

"Sure," said Harold. "Think it over and get back to me. If things are looking bad there for you, maybe I can help out."

"Thanks, Harold," said Nadia. "I appreciate that."

"Sure thing," Harold replied. "Anyway, thanks for the update. We'll be in touch with you about the budget shortly."

"Stacy," corrected Nadia. "Get in touch with Stacy on that one."

"Right," said Harold. "Stacy. Thanks again, Nadia. Have a great evening."

"You, too."

Nadia hung up the phone and slid it down onto the coffee table. She gave a big, dramatic sigh and looked absently into her computer screen for a moment. Harold made an enticing offer, but Nadia still felt committed to Avery even though they had no concrete plans. She found herself falling for Avery. Maybe it was the new relationship honeymoon period — they had only been together a few months — but it felt so good and so real and Nadia was starting to believe that she was in love with Avery. How could she leave now?

Noticing the time, Nadia shut her laptop and stood up. She stretched out and then shook her arms out, trying to inspire a burst of energy. Dressed down for the evening in just a skimpy pair of running shorts and a thin t-shirt, Nadia slipped into her flip-flops, she grabbed a six pack of beer from the refrigerator, and then she walked down the hall to meet up with Laurie.

Together Nadia and Laurie sat on a picnic table on the roof of their building, both looking relaxed in light clothes and sunglasses. They each held a bottle of beer in their hands. The uncertainty they had felt initially about their jobs had faded into acceptance as the summer rolled in. It didn't really bother them anymore.

"So, I got the job," said Laurie, taking a swig of her beer. She smiled happily and Nadia smiled as well.

"That's so great!" said Nadia. "Congratulations." She held up her bottle and they clinked them together.

"I'm going to miss working with you," Laurie continued. "I'm sad that you're not coming with me to Digimedia."

"Agreed," Nadia replied. "It's the end of an era."

"At least we live in the same building," Laurie said, smiling hopefully.

"I just got a job offer, too," said Nadia. "Well, sort of a half job offer."

"When?" said Laurie. "Just now?"

"Before we came up here," said Nadia. "I was talking to Harold at Polly and he was trying to convince me to move out to California and work for them."

"You're kidding!" boasted Laurie. "Nadia, that's insane. Work at Polly? That's a huge deal."

"I mean, it *is* a pretty big deal," said Nadia.

"Are you going to do it?" said Laurie. "I don't want to lose you, of course, but that's really a job you need to explore. That could be a huge move for you."

"I don't know," said Nadia. "To be honest, things are going really well with Avery. I'm not sure I want to leave her just as our relationship is really getting off the ground."

"Sure, but don't you think she'll go back to New York when this is all over?" asked Laurie. "That's her home. She's only in Chicago for a short time. Another six months, and she could be gone. You don't want to pass up this Polly offer, get laid off from Color Wheel, and then find out your girlfriend is leaving you to go back to her old life across the country."

"I guess I didn't think about it like that," said Nadia. She ruminated on Laurie's words, and she drank from her bottle. What Laurie said made perfect sense, and Nadia felt a little naive for being so blind to it.

"I think you've really got to think about yourself in this one," said Laurie. "I know you and Avery are talking about going into business together somehow, but you don't really have any concrete plans."

"That's true," Nadia said.

"And if I'm being honest," Laurie went on. "These corporate types can be sociopaths. I'm not calling Avery a sociopath necessarily," she said, holding up her palm. "I'm just saying that sometimes their sense of what's acceptable — *emotionally* — is a bit skewed. It's all about the bottom line for them."

"You don't really think Avery is like that, do you?" Nadia questioned, really taking Laurie's words to heart.

"I said I'm not calling her a sociopath," said Laurie. "But people in her position, they get conditioned by doing things based on money rather than based on what's good for the people involved. I think it can mess with a person's mind. When her job is over here in Chicago, she might think it's okay to just break up with you and move on."

"I don't know," said Nadia. "I think she really likes me, too. I think that things are really developing between us."

"I hope that's true," Laurie said with an empathetic smile. "But just to be safe, don't let this possibility with Polly slip between your fingers. It's a good opportunity for you. It could really propel your career. But I would so hate to see you leave me," she said, reaching across the table, gripping onto Nadia's hand, and offering her a loving smile. Nadia smiled back.

"I know you're right," Nadia acquiesced, squeezing back on her friend's hand. "I should look out for myself."

"If you don't, who will?" said Laurie. "It's rough out there. There's so little security, it feels like you've really got to pave your own way."

"That's how I feel, too," said Nadia. "And that's why I've really been thinking about doing my own thing. With Avery. I don't want to end up in another position like what's happened at Color Wheel. I don't want to work my ass off for something only to have it pulled out from under me. And Avery is going through the same thing. She really thought she had a shot as CEO of Scheffler & Vonn. But they're getting rid of her, just as they're getting rid of Color Wheel."

"Polly's not like Color Wheel," said Laurie. Then she

held up her cell phone. "They're ubiquitous. And they're only getting bigger. It could really be a big deal for you."

"I'm going to think about it," said Nadia. "I'm going to think about what you said. I don't ever want to be in this situation again. And I don't want to get my heart broken."

"You've got a good head on your shoulders, Nadia," said Laurie, smiling wide. "I'm so glad that we've become such good friends. I promise I'd come out to California to visit you."

"Thanks," said Nadia, laughing, and then taking a drink. Nadia knew that she had a lot to consider. Things were evolving and she had to evolve with them. While she honestly did feel love for Avery, she needed to know that Avery's intentions were true. She needed to know that this was the real deal and not just a convenient relationship for a rich, jet-setting executive. And if they were to continue their professional lives together, if that wasn't just some ruse, Nadia felt like they really needed to have a plan. Otherwise, she would have to focus on any other offers that came her way. Her time at Color Wheel was almost up.

Nadia needed something more.

<hr />

WITH HER LAPTOP bag slung over her shoulder, Nadia walked into Avery's building in Streeterville and approached the desk. She smiled at the attendant, a man in a dark blue suit named James, and when he noticed her, he smiled back.

"Good evening, Miss Marek," said James. "Is Miss Wool expecting you?"

"She is," said Nadia, patting her bag. "I'm here to do a little bit of work."

"Then I won't bother calling up," he said. "You can go right ahead."

"Thanks, James," said Nadia. "Have a great evening."

"You do the same."

Nadia made her way to the bank of elevators and walked inside the first one to open. She hit Avery's floor, and the doors slid closed. The elevator began to ascend with a low, dull hum. Nadia smiled at herself, reflected in the mirror-finished interior walls of the elevator and she delicately fussed with her hair. She was always excited to see Avery. Despite the uncertainty she felt, Nadia truly felt like she was falling for her. Maybe the uncertainty made it all the more exciting.

Once she arrived at Avery's floor, she ambled casually down the hall, familiar with the building by now and happy to be closing in on her lover's apartment. Nadia approached Avery's door and knocked on it firmly, a pleased and happy look on her face.

After a moment, the door swung open to reveal a sullen Avery. As soon as Nadia saw her, her excitement and happiness distorted into worry and fear. Avery was not as well-dressed or made-up as she usually was. She appeared as though she might have been crying before Nadia had arrived.

"Avery," said Nadia tenderly. "Are you okay?"

"Yes, I am," said Avery. She stepped out of the way and waved Nadia in. Nadia slowly entered and watched as Avery shut the door behind her.

"I hope I didn't surprise you," Nadia continued, removing her bag and setting it atop a small table in the entranceway. "James didn't think he needed to call up and—"

"Oh, don't worry about that," said Avery. "Of course I'm happy to see you." She stepped closer to Nadia and the women embraced. Avery held on tightly, and she pushed her face into Nadia's neck as though she were trying to hide from her.

"If something's wrong," said Nadia. "You can tell me about it. Or if you'd rather I just leave, that's okay, too."

Avery was silent for a few more moments. Then she slowly stood upright and stepped back from Nadia. She smiled softly and then wiped at her eye.

"It's all happening," said Avery. "Much quicker than anticipated."

"What's all happening?"

"Color Wheel's days are numbered," said Avery. "And so are mine."

"You're kidding?" said Nadia. "I thought Frances had built some sort of timeline into the contract."

"Oh, Nadia," said Avery. "Scheffler & Vonn never would have agreed to terms like that if they weren't also sure they could weasel out of them. There's nothing Frances can do about it. It's over, darling. It's all over."

"So what does this mean for you?" Nadia asked. "Once Color Wheels shutters its doors?"

"I don't know," said Avery. "They've pushed me off of the board and have told me that if I return to the corporate offices I will have to accept a lower level management position. It's really just a convenient way to make me quit, because they know there's no way someone at my level would accept such a role. It would be horrible for my career. So, I suppose, once Color Wheel closes, I will be quitting Scheffler & Vonn."

Avery sighed and she quickly turned from Nadia, walking into the kitchen and picking up a rocks glass that was already on the counter. It was half full of whiskey, and Avery took a drink from it. Nadia followed her and leaned up against the counter. She was full of questions, but Avery was obviously not in a very good place, and so Nadia knew she had to be sensitive.

"Will you be staying here?" Nadia said. "In Chicago, I mean?"

"I will no longer have access to this condo," said Avery. "It's paid for by the company. And my home is in New York."

"So you're going to leave?" said Nadia carefully. "You're going to leave me?"

"I just don't know," replied Avery. She looked at Nadia and she smiled gently. "I don't want to leave you. But my connection to this city is very tenuous."

"Were you crying?" Nadia asked, her voice soft and caring.

"Me?" said Avery, wiping at her eye again. "No, I wasn't. Do I look like I was crying?"

"Yes."

"Well, maybe I was," said Avery. "Maybe just a little bit. I just worked so hard for this. I don't know where I went wrong."

"You know," said Nadia. "A lot of people in the office feel like that, too. We've all worked hard, dedicated ourselves to this, and now it's being taken away from us. And they look to you like you're the one who's ruining their livelihood, but you're experiencing the exact same thing."

"Ironic, isn't it?" Avery countered with a weak smile. "I'm not some monster who can't feel empathy. I know my role has been dastardly from the beginning. But it was my job. And yet, it didn't get me any closer to the goal I was after." She took a big gulp of her whiskey and she winced.

"You shouldn't go," Nadia said. She stepped around the kitchen island and closer to Avery. "Even if Color Wheel shuts down, you should stay here in Chicago."

"You want me to stay?" said Avery. A small smile crept over her. "You know, all this time, I couldn't help but feel like, on some level, you resented me. It's always been in the back of my mind. I know that's silly, but I've felt guilty. I've lead the charge in ridding you of your job." Avery laughed sadly, took another drink, and then smiled at Nadia.

"It would be pretty easy to resent you in that regard," said Nadia. "But I don't feel that way. I've known all along that you were just doing your job. And once I saw more of your situation, I began to understand the power struggles and see what you've been dealing with in your own life."

"I appreciate that so much," said Avery. She embraced Nadia and held her close. "I really do. It isn't easy doing what I do. I don't get a sick thrill out of it. It hurts, but I've had to remain strong if I wanted to have a shot at CEO of the company. Those dreams are over now."

"It's okay," said Nadia. She pressed a tender kiss to Avery's lips and Avery, as though she were attention starved, eagerly returned the kiss. The two stood there in silence, kissing sweet kiss after sweet kiss, the only thing that could be heard was the resounding noise of lips smacking echoing throughout the kitchen.

Nadia smiled as she stepped back, hands resting on Avery's hips, and she looked at Avery in the eyes. Avery was already looking brighter and happier.

"I brought my computer," Nadia said after another moment. "Do you want to work tonight? We can keep brainstorming ideas for a possible joint business."

"Let's just order sushi and drink this whiskey," said Avery. She tossed her head back and drank the rest of the booze in her glass. "And then we'll have a tipsy roll in the sheets." Nadia laughed.

"I can get on board with that," Nadia replied.

"Thank you for understanding me, Nadia," said Avery. "It can be quite lonely where I am. People are always so cautious if they're under you. And if they're over you, well, it's like you don't matter at all."

"It doesn't have to be like that," said Nadia. "You don't have to exist in that world."

"I believe it's my fate," Avery said with a mysticism in her voice. "Some of us must fill this role. We're born into it, in a way. Where I come from, I certainly was. There's no stepping back."

"Well, maybe you can change the game," said Nadia. "Maybe when you run your own business, it won't be so cutthroat."

"Maybe," said Avery wistfully. She paused. "My father and my brother arrived today. Will you be available to do lunch tomorrow with us?"

"Yes," said Nadia, smiling happily. It made her feel good to know that Avery wanted her to join, even though she was slightly nervous to meet Avery's family. "I would really love that."

"Good," said Avery. "I already told them you were coming. I told them you were a potential business partner, and that the two of us had been dating."

"A business partner?" Nadia said, laughing incredulously. "Doesn't that make it seem like I have money to invest? I definitely don't."

"Oh, don't be silly," said Avery. "You will have your sweat equity. As soon as we can figure out what course we're going to take."

"I'm going to get my computer," said Nadia, turning from Avery and returning to the entryway to retrieve her bag. "If we're meeting with your family tomorrow, we should have a business to talk about. We should do at least a little bit of work."

"And then sushi, yes?" asked Avery.

"Yes," said Nadia, returning with a smile. "Then sushi."

"And drinks and sex?"

"All of that, too," said Nadia. "You pour."

Avery smiled big and nodded. She removed a glass from the cupboard for Nadia, and she filled the glasses to the halfway point. Handing one glass over to Nadia, Avery took the other for herself and lifted it up.

They clinked glasses. And they drank.

THE FOUR OF them sat together at a steakhouse on the river. The wall of windows, looking out to the river and to the skyscrapers in the Loop, was open and warm summer air flitted in from outdoors. It was an obviously upper-class crowd, many men in suits and women in dresses, along with some tourists who had read the positive reviews about the restaurant. Avery and Nadia sat on one side of the table, while Avery's father Charles and her brother Max sat on the opposite side.

Nadia smiled as she took a bite of her steak, mostly content to just listen in to the conversation rather than try to contribute. She felt slightly out of place in this restaurant, and among the Wool family, but she took it in stride. As her relationship with Avery progressed, she could feel herself growing more confident but she still had a long way to go.

Despite the success in her career, she hadn't yet reached the level of business that was represented by the people at this table. She was happy, though, to have the experience.

"The building is on South Clark Street," said Charles, who must have been in his early 70s. His hair was grey, full, and well-manicured. He looked quite healthy for his age. "We currently have negotiated slightly below their asking price and are close to settling at eighty-six million."

Nadia's eyes widened at talk of such a large number, but she kept her mouth closed and was content to remain a fly on the wall.

"It's a good first step into the Chicago market," said Max. "We hope to acquire a few more buildings here over the course of the next handful of years."

"How much of the building is currently leased?" Avery asked with interest.

"Eighty-four percent," said Max. "Average lease term is around five years, and in-place rents are eighteen percent below market rates. Plenty of room to expand rent spreads."

"This sounds like a good purchase," said Avery. "And that's a good price."

"We have our eyes on other buildings downtown," said Charles. "But we'll have to raise more capital before we can leap into the more desirable buildings in the city."

"So where do I come in?" Avery said. "How can I help?"

"Seeing as you're already in Chicago for work," said Max. "We were hoping that you could setup an office in the building once the sale goes through so that we may transition management over to our group."

"Max and I will be completing the purchase from afar," said Charles. "We're only here currently for a tour of the building before we agree to the terms."

"Of course, if it's too much to ask," said Max. "We wouldn't want your work to suffer with Scheffler & Vonn, but we could really use your expertise for this project."

Avery took it all in, and she nodded slowly. Her eyes looked over to Nadia, who returned the look for support. It seemed as though Avery was looking for some kind of sign, like she was trying to make a decision and she was searching for the answer within Nadia. After a moment, Nadia smiled and Avery smiled back.

"Well," Avery begun, trying to find the appropriate words that would save face in front of her successful family. "As it happens, my time at Scheffler & Vonn is winding down. So, too, my own project here in Chicago."

"Your time at Scheffler & Vonn is winding down," Charles repeated. "What does that mean, Avery? Are you leaving your position?"

"I'm no longer needed, it appears," she replied, remaining strong and confident. "Which is just as well, because I had been growing tired of the atmosphere there. And the opportunities I wanted just weren't available to me."

Charles and Max looked to each other and then back to Avery.

"Dear," said Charles. "You know you're always welcome

back at M. M. Wool. If you no longer have your position with Scheffler & Vonn, you should come and work for us once again."

"We'd love to have you back, Avery," said Max. "We certainly have other projects that could use your expertise."

"For this project," said Avery. "The building here in Chicago. I will assist in any way that I can. But as for the future, I'm just not sure. I have a lot to consider before I make any decisions."

"Understood," said Charles. "I will say, however, that we've missed you. I've missed you," he said, offering his daughter a warm smile. Avery returned the smile and she nodded.

"I was wondering," said Avery, once again looking over toward Nadia. "Nadia's job is also coming to an end. Would there be any opportunity for her with M. M. Wool if that was something she was interested in?"

Nadia looked to Avery in surprise, as this wasn't something they had discussed. She didn't know how to feel about the question, and she tried not to panic.

"That depends," said Charles, offering a smile at Nadia. "Nadia, can you tell us a little bit about yourself?"

"Um, sure," said Nadia. "Well, I've been working for the advertising agency here in Chicago that Avery recently took over for about seven years. I started as a graphic designer, but eventually took over a management role. I've worked with large, multinational clients, such as Polly, the smartphone manufacturer."

"Yes, I have one of their phones," said Charles.

"I do, as well," said Max.

"I was their account manager and I also did some creative direction," Nadia continued, trying to be as professional as she could. "But things have changed at the company since Scheffler & Vonn took over, so that part of my responsibility is, well, going away."

"Do you have any experience with property management or real estate?" Charles asked.

"I own a condo," Nadia said and smiled sheepishly. Charles and Max smiled.

"If my daughter recommends you for employment," said Charles. "I would certainly place your application at the top of the pile. We can always use bright, hard-working young people to help take this company into the future."

"I appreciate that, sir," said Nadia.

There were more smiles around the table.

Lunch continued on with more business talk, and Nadia mostly stayed out of it. But she was keen to listen. Avery really knew her stuff, and it was obvious that her family was trying to court her back, especially so after they discovered that she was in need of a job. There was hesitance in Avery's voice, though, like she wasn't sure if she wanted to return to her family company. She told her father she would definitely consider it, and that she needed to do some thinking.

Once the lunch ended, Charles and Max needing to leave for a meeting, Avery and Nadia exited the steakhouse and decided to take a stroll along the riverside before they headed back to the Color Wheel offices. They walked side by side, the cool breeze coming off the river offering a respite from the summer heat. It felt relaxing and easy.

"What's your hesitation?" asked Nadia. "If you're going to leave Scheffler & Vonn, why not just go back to working with your family?"

"I always pictured myself as a high-powered CEO," admitted Avery. "In an industry with a bit more flash. Advertising or publishing, or even in film and television. Real estate investment and property management, it's just not as exciting. And I'll never be CEO at M. M. Wool. That job will be Max's eventually."

"Is it just that your father is sexist?" said Nadia carefully. "Is that why you were never in line for CEO?"

Avery sighed and stopped.

"Well, no," Avery said after a moment of pause. "He always preferred that whoever took over for him was a lawyer. It's important to have a lawyer's eyes on these large real estate deals, as the contracts can get very complex. But I never wanted to go to law school."

"Oh," said Nadia, feeling like Avery was finally truly beginning to open up to her. "And Max…"

"He's a lawyer," said Avery. "I got my MBA, but never a JD. That's why I will not be taking over M. M. Wool Properties."

"You know, maybe it's not so bad that you don't," said Nadia. "There's nothing wrong with *not* becoming a high-powered CEO. You don't need that title to be happy."

"I have felt for a very long time that I indeed *did* need that title to be happy," said Avery. "But now that I'm being pushed out of Scheffler & Vonn, I'm not so sure what I want anymore."

Nadia smiled and she took Avery's hand. She squeezed, and she looked into Avery's eyes. Avery smiled and squeezed back.

"Happiness is about more than a job," said Nadia. "And it's not just some place in the future. We can be happy right now."

"I am happy right now," said Avery. She was still smiling, looking into Nadia's eyes. Both women could feel the intensity brewing between them. It felt right. It felt like this was something special.

"I am, too," said Nadia. Stepping closer to her lover, Nadia pressed her own lips tenderly against Avery's. And Avery eagerly accepted. They stood there on the riverside for some time, delicately kissing one another, feeling as though time had stopped. Beyond this kiss, nothing else mattered. It was the only thing that existed in the world.

"Thank you for understanding me," Avery said in a whisper as their kiss came to an end. Her face lingered close to Nadia's, as though she was hovering near in adoration.

Nadia knew something had changed in that moment. Something really big. Any kind of barrier left between her and Avery had crumbled and they were now closer than ever. It was special and, Nadia was certain, it was love.

A FEW WEEKS LATER, Nadia was sitting in her office, holding

the phone to her ear, and feeling as though it had become rather pointless for her to come in to work at all. Stacy in New York had taken most of her higher level work away from her, the overall sentiment in the office was depressed, Laurie had already left for her new job, and most of Nadia's coworkers had come to hate the woman she loved. It was obvious what was happening, and employees were beginning to jump ship. This had become the stereotypical corporate buy-out, and they all knew it.

But Nadia was unsure what she was going to do next. There was the offer from Harold at Polly in California, though Nadia felt in her gut that it wasn't the right move for her. There was still a chance she could follow Laurie to Digi-media. And there was the possibility of working with Avery at M. M. Wool, which fascinated Nadia but she was unsure what to think about it. She had options, but they all felt very hazy. Still, she knew she had to do something, she had to make some move, or else she would be stuck with nothing when Color Wheel finally shut its doors.

The only thing Nadia was certain of was her feelings for Avery. Nadia adored her, and her feelings only became greater as the women grew to know each other more. Avery wasn't like anybody she had met before. It felt as though she was on a higher plain. She was smarter, more confident, stronger. Avery was a unique soul, and she was the kind of woman Nadia had always pictured herself becoming but could never quite get there.

As Nadia thought about Avery, she appeared as if out of nowhere in the doorway with a curious smile on her face.

When Nadia saw her, she couldn't help but smile back. Nadia eagerly waved her in, and Avery entered the small office, closing the door behind her.

"It's brutal in this office," Avery admitted, walking close to Nadia's desk and then sitting on top of it. She hung her legs over the side next to where Nadia sat. Avery wore a pencil skirt, and her legs were bare, silky, soft. She adjusted her skirt and got comfortable.

"I'm sorry," said Nadia. "I know it is. I think everybody is desperately looking for new jobs."

"Yes, and shooting daggers at me," said Avery. She sighed and then smiled and fluffed her hair. "If only they knew that I was in the same boat."

"You could tell them," offered Nadia. "You could tell them that you've essentially lost your job, too."

"That won't do anything to make them feel better," said Avery. "And when you're captain of the ship, you never let the crew members see your panic, even if that ship is sinking."

"It will be okay," said Nadia. Leaning down, she placed a gentle kiss on Avery's leg. Avery grinned.

"Further up," Avery replied.

Nadia smiled, and she kissed Avery's leg once again, this time closer to the hemline of her skirt.

"Further up still," said Avery.

"It appears I'm thwarted by this fabric," said Nadia, giving a teasing tug at Avery's skirt.

"I could take it off if you like," Avery said, a fire coming alive in her eyes.

"I wish," said Nadia. "I'm so bored here. I've got no work to do. I'm just sitting in my office staring at my computer screen, hoping for an email to pop in. But there's nothing."

"Then let's do it," Avery said with a shrug. "Take off my skirt and let's have some fun." Nadia could tell from Avery's expression that she was serious.

"Here?" Nadia replied skeptically. "Someone could knock on my door at any second. You're crazy."

"Okay," Avery said, hopping up from the desk. "Is there some place in the office we can go to be alone?"

"There's the old lounge on the other side of the office," said Nadia. "Nobody's really working on that side anymore and the door locks."

"Let's go," said Avery, taking hold of Nadia's arm and pulling her to her feet. "I'm feeling frisky."

Nadia felt her heart start to beat faster and she smiled excitedly.

After a walk through the office in which both women tried to act completely normal, they found themselves in a small lounge room that had really only been used lately for people to make private personal calls. There was a more natural, and dimmer, light in this room, meant to be a respite from the fluorescent lights that illuminated the rest of the office. There was a big plush leather couch on one side, a small table, and two chairs that matched the couch against the opposite wall. It was a comfortable room, quiet, and Nadia and Avery, now barefoot, lay on the couch together, wrapped up in one another, slowly making out while their hands explored each other's body.

An eager Nadia quickly found herself reaching a hand up Avery's skirt, and pressing her fingers against her lover. She could feel Avery's buoyancy, her wetness, and a few hairs poking through the thin fabric of her panties. Nadia rubbed back and forth and Avery purred against her. Their kissing grew more heated as the groping became more passionate.

"Have you ever fooled around at work before?" Avery asked between kisses.

"No," admitted Nadia. "But I like it."

"I wish you wouldn't have worn pants today," Avery said, grabbing at the waist of Nadia's pants and trying to quickly undo the clasp. It didn't take her long before she had pulled Nadia's zipper down, and she too buried her hand between Nadia's leg. Nadia squirmed in delight.

"God, I'm so hot for you," cooed Nadia. She kissed Avery's neck and closed her eyes as she felt Avery's fingers explore. Nadia wished she could just snap her fingers and the two of them could magically be completely naked.

Just then, there was a jiggle of the door handle and then a quick and abrupt knock at the door. The women both stopped dead and looked to one another with wide eyes. Nadia could feel her heart beat go double-time.

"Hello?" said a muffled voice from the other side. "Is anybody in there?"

"Yes!" Avery called back. "We are in a meeting and we shouldn't be longer than an hour."

"I apologize," said the voice. And then there was silence. Nadia and Avery continued looking at one another, listening for any other sounds. After they were sure that the interloper had left, they both sighed in relief.

"Holy shit," said Avery. The expression on her face grew even more passionate. "It's hot to be almost caught."

"It is," agreed Nadia, who immediately resumed her passion, pressing her lips to Avery's and bringing the lust in the room back to an even greater level than before.

It wasn't much longer before Avery's underwear, a thin and lacy swatch of fabric, was on the floor, her skirt was hiked up higher on her thighs, and Nadia had her hand between her legs, pumping back and forth. Nadia could feel Avery clenching sporadically to her two inserted fingers, and she methodically moved them in and out, easily gliding through Avery's wet flesh.

"Oh, that's so good," moaned Avery near Nadia's ear. The timbre of Avery's voice made the light hair on Nadia's arms stand on end. Making her lover feel pleasured brought pleasure to Nadia herself, and she could feel an eager dampness between her own thighs. Never before had Nadia pictured herself being in such a situation, but now that she was experiencing it, she wished she had done it sooner.

And when Avery finally came, Nadia could feel an increased wetness on her hand. She couldn't help but massage it into Avery's flesh and fur, rubbing her soaked hand back and forth against her lover's tenderness as Avery squirmed and cooed and held tightly to Nadia. As Avery began to cool and relax, Nadia removed her hand from between Avery's legs and raised it up so she could see it.

"Wow," mused Nadia, looking at her hand. Her fingers with tacky and viscous, creamed with a subtle milky whiteness. "You were really wet." Avery laughed and lightly smacked Nadia, her face looking as though she were in a daze.

"When I get really turned on," said Avery. "It gets messy down there."

"I like it," said Nadia, still inspecting her hand. After a moment she popped her fingers into her mouth and sucked Avery's juices off. Avery laughed happily.

"Now that's hot," Avery remarked. "I'm going to file that image away in my mind so that I can call it up the next time I'm pleasuring myself."

Nadia, feeling playful, stuck just one of her fingers out and slowly licked it as though she were performing a show for Avery. It obviously made Avery quite happy.

"It's your turn," said Avery, rolling off of Nadia and standing up from the couch. Her skirt was still hiked up and Nadia could see the matted hair of Avery's wet bush. "Take off your pants and spread your legs."

Nadia earnestly obeyed, swiftly shimmying out of her dress slacks where she lay on the couch as Avery watched with yearning enthusiasm in her eyes. All Nadia could think about was the impending touch of her lover. It was all she cared about, and it was everything.

Work no longer seemed to matter.

NADIA SAT upright on the edge of the couch in Avery's rented condo. She was naked, fresh out of the shower, and she was leaned over her knee, foot propped against the coffee table, applying a clear coat to her toenails. Something was truly beginning to change inside of her. Where she was once overly concerned about her work life, she had now discovered a new sense of ease within herself. She liked it. This new demeanor made her feel a bit more free, and it was a welcome change from the workaholic she once was.

There was more to life than work. And Nadia was truly beginning to see that.

Avery sauntered in from the other room, wearing a silk robe that hung open at her chest, barely covering her breasts as she sashayed into the kitchen with her phone pressed to her ear.

"It's over," she said firmly into the phone. "There's very little left for me to do, Martin, and I have another job offer that I must entertain." Avery paused near the kitchen island and leaned against it, taking up a glass of water that had been sitting there and drank from it. "Yes, I understand," she went on when it was her turn to speak. "But if Scheffler & Vonn refuses to be loyal to me, there's not much else I can do. It's time to move on."

Nadia watched Avery with interest, a small smile across her lips. Avery was such a confident woman, so unafraid, and it simultaneously filled Nadia with envy and turned her on.

Darting her eyes over, Avery caught Nadia looking at her and, as a tease, she yanked open one lapel of her robe to expose a breast for Nadia to see. Then she grinned, covered herself back up, and returned to her conversation.

"I regret that as well, Martin," Avery said. "But if you want someone to strip the place for copper to sell, I am not your woman. I am content to part ways now and forget this whole debacle ever happened." She paused as Martin spoke. "Yes, I do plan to vacate. I will be out of this apartment within a week and you may send whichever flunky you like to take over. I'm finished."

Avery switched ears with her phone and listened. Her eyes looked back and forth between Nadia, who was still watching her, and whatever else she could connect with in the condo as she listened to her now former boss speak. She covered the microphone with her other hand and grumbled a few expletives before returning to the conversation.

"Your non-compete can shove it, and you know very well it's unenforceable," said Avery. "Who do you take me for? Again, I'm finished, Martin. Please send me whatever paperwork you need me to sign. And you're welcome for the years I put in here. It was my mistake. Goodbye."

Avery hung up her phone and slid it onto the island.

"These fucking people," she said, shaking her head. Avery languidly ambled across the room and toward where Nadia sat on the couch. "I probably didn't handle that the best I could, but here we are." She smiled and put her hands on her hips, looking down at Nadia.

Nadia smiled an easy, pretty smile.

"You're gorgeous," said Avery. "Sitting there naked on my couch. Well, formally my couch. Why don't you just lay back and let me do what I'm best at."

"Can't you see I'm painting my toenails?" said Nadia with a sly grin. "Why don't you show me your tit again?"

"You mean this tit?" asked Avery, once again quickly flashing Nadia.

"That's the one," said Nadia. Avery laughed.

"It's good to know I've still got it," said Avery. She sat down on the arm of the couch and smiled. "I suppose all good things must come to an end. I don't know what came over me. I suppose I was just tired of being pushed around, knowing that my time was short anyway."

"It's all right," said Nadia, as she put her other foot up on the coffee table and continued on with her toes. "I'm sure you'll be fine. You don't strike me as the kind of woman who will have difficulty finding another job."

"You are correct," said Avery. "But I still have that project to do for my family. And now I have no apartment."

"You can come stay with me," said Nadia. She offered Avery an accepting smile.

"Yes?" said Avery. "Well, that's very kind of you."

"If you can slum it in a not-as-nice place," Nadia continued on, grinning to herself as she focused on her nails.

"So that's what you think of me," said Avery. "It all comes out. Heap on the pretentious rich lady, is that it?"

"My condo is in no way as nice as this place," Nadia

continued on. "Nor is it even close enough to sniff your home in New York."

"Well, maybe I *won't* stay with you," said Avery, batting at her hair and looking away in mock-anger. "Maybe I'll just find another posh furnished condo where I can be snobby all by myself."

Nadia put the cap on her polish and set it on the table. Then she leaned back on the couch, both feet up on the table, so that her entire body was exposed. She put her hands behind her head and she smiled, wiggling her toes.

"On second thought," said Avery, scanning her lover up and down. "Maybe I will take you up on your offer. Only until I get back on my feet, you understand."

"Sure, sure," said Nadia.

"You're a trip," said Avery, slipping down off the arm and sitting her rear next to Nadia. Her robe opened up ever so slightly so that more of her chest could be seen. Nadia peeked in and grinned.

"Of course you can stay with me," said Nadia, finally breaking the tease. "I would love to have you over." Dropping her hand, she placed it on Avery's bare thigh and caressed back and forth.

"When I first agreed to take over as CEO at Color Wheel and come to Chicago," said Avery. "I never imagined that this is where I would end up."

"Where's that?"

"Leaving my job and joining up with you," said Avery. "It's certainly been a surprising twist of fate." Leaning over, she kissed Nadia delicately.

"I guess I'm the same," said Nadia. "I didn't think I'd be at the tail end of my job, together with someone like you, and... surprisingly cool with no idea what might happen next." She laughed at herself, and Avery smiled wide.

"Why don't you join me for this project for my family?" asked Avery. "You never know, you might enjoy it."

"I might," said Nadia. "But I feel a bit under qualified for that kind of thing."

"Oh stop," said Avery. "You're a brilliant woman with a keen work ethic. I think you'll thrive anywhere."

"Maybe," Nadia replied, her smile growing.

"But you don't plan to go to California, do you?" said Avery. "Have you made any decisions about that?"

"I just don't think I can do it," said Nadia. "I love it here in Chicago. I'm sure California is nice, but this is my home. I grew up here. This is where I want to be."

"Next week I will be meeting with some of M. M. Wool's partners in this building deal," said Avery. "Join me."

"Yeah?"

"Yes," said Avery. "We'll dress very serious and proper and have a good time of it. You just follow my lead and I think we'll do fine."

"Okay," Nadia agreed. "I'm in. But if I ruin the deal, I am not responsible for it."

"I will take the heat for you, darling," Avery said. They kissed. And then they kissed again.

Their lazy kissing grew more passionate as they sat against one another there on the couch. Soon, Avery had slipped her hand between Nadia's legs and was adoringly combing her fingers through Nadia's bush. Nadia was brimming with happiness at Avery's touch, and she braced herself against Avery by holding her hand against Avery's arm. She widened her legs slightly as if to tell Avery she could do whatever she wanted.

After a few moments of kissing, Avery pulled back and the women opened their eyes and smiled at one another. This felt right, and it felt real. Nadia could feel the emotion welling up inside of her, and without thinking twice about it, she opened her mouth.

"I love you," said Nadia.

"I love you, too," Avery replied.

"I'll help you move," Nadia went on.

"Lucky that I didn't bring many things with me," Avery said. "This apartment came furnished." She smiled and she kissed Nadia once again.

"I'm glad you're here in Chicago," said Nadia.

"So am I." They kissed, and Nadia could feel it in her heart.

They still had an adventure in front of them, and Nadia was happy to share it with someone like Avery. She certainly was a complex woman, very tough on the exterior but soft and passionate when she needed to be. It was like a secret version of Avery that only Nadia was privy to. And that filled her with joy. In fact, any time she was around Avery, all she could feel was joy. It was a great feeling.

THREE

$\mathcal{L}$aurie walked down the hallway with a bottle of wine in her hand. She had an easy smile on her face, the kind of smile you get when you finally get home from work on a Friday evening after a long week. Her new job had kept her busy, and it had been a little while since she and Nadia had gotten the chance to hang out. But now that the weekend had arrived, Laurie was ready to finally reconnect with her friend.

She approached Nadia's door and she knocked a tune. It took a moment, but soon Laurie heard the lock unlatching and then the door swung open. Laurie was surprised to see who was on the other side.

"Avery," said Laurie. "How are you?"

"Just fine," said Avery. "I'm very well. And how are you?"

"I'm great," Laurie said, feeling a hint of confusion. Avery was more dressed down than Laurie had ever seen her, wearing a pair of cotton lounge shorts and a tank top. She hardly looked like the Avery that Laurie had once known, always dressed in business attire and perfectly made-up.

"Would you like to come in?" Avery said with a smile. "Nadia just stepped out to pick up some wine and I was straightening up in here."

"Sure," said Laurie gingerly, walking inside of Nadia's condo as Avery stepped out of her way. "I brought wine if you'd like to have a glass," she said, presenting the bottle to Avery.

"Lovely," said Avery, taking the bottle from her. She moved toward the kitchen and Laurie followed her, still feeling wildly uncertain about the situation. Although she knew that there was romance between Nadia and Avery, it still felt odd to be standing there alone with her former boss.

"Is Nadia going to be back shortly?" Laurie asked with trepidation.

"Does it make you uncomfortable to be here with just me?" Avery said with a teasing grin.

"Well, no…" Laurie said. "I just… I was hoping to catch up with Nadia."

"Ah," said Avery, popping the cork on the wine and pouring two glasses. She smiled and handed one to Laurie. "I'm sure she's on her way home."

"Thank you," said Laurie, accepting the glass and taking a sip.

"You know," said Avery, leaning her hip against the kitchen island and taking a drink. "I hope you don't hold any grudges against me. For all that unfortunate stuff that went down."

"You mean buying out the company I enjoyed working for and shutting it down?" Laurie said with a hint of sarcasm. "No, of course not."

"That's rather glib," said Avery. "But it's a very simplistic way of looking at it."

"I know," Laurie admitted, sighing and taking another drink. "I know it's not like you personally did all of that. The wounds are still fresh, though, you know?"

"I was in the same boat," said Avery. "Just as you were forced out of your job, so was I. I no longer work for Scheffler & Vonn. I'm a free agent, as it were."

"Yes, Nadia told me," said Laurie. "Sometimes it feels like it's all just a big game. But it's like, no matter how good you get at playing the game, you still have very little control in how it plays out."

"I think that's an apt description," said Avery. "Even those of us who think we've mastered it still lose sometimes."

"I have to admit," said Laurie. "It's very weird to see you not in some kind of suit." Avery looked down at herself and laughed.

"I am a person as well," Avery teased. "And I'm embracing a more relaxed lifestyle, at Nadia's insistence. I'm enjoying it."

"That's good," Laurie said and smiled.

"I have a tendency to be a workaholic," admitted Avery. "And when a person is a workaholic, they take everything concerning their work very seriously. A little too seriously at points. Sometimes it feels like even when you do your best, it's never enough."

"I think you and Nadia are cut from the same cloth," replied Laurie.

"I agree," said Avery. "And I think that's what drew us together."

"Have either of you made any work decisions yet?" asked Laurie. Just as she proposed this question, the door unlocked and Nadia stepped inside the condo smiling big. She held a canvas bag in one hand, with a few bottles of wine inside of it that clinked when she moved, and she was dressed in casual summer garb. When Nadia noticed Laurie was there, her smile grew even larger and she jogged over to welcome her friend.

"Hey, babe," said Nadia, hugging Laurie, the bag still dangling from her hand. She squeezed tightly.

"Hey," said Laurie, returning the hug. "I've missed you."

"Yeah, you've been totally MIA lately," said Nadia, stepping back and beginning to remove the wine bottles from her bag, placing them on the counter.

"I'm sorry," Laurie said. "Digimedia has been a whirlwind. I mean, I'm loving it, but they've really kept me busy."

"We've been the opposite lately," said Nadia, looking to Avery and smiling. "Just trying to enjoy the summer. Avery was able to orchestrate a severance for me at Color Wheel, so I've just been giving myself some time to figure out what's next."

Laurie looked to Avery and offered her an appreciative smile, and Avery returned it.

"So you're not stressed about money?" said Laurie. "That's great."

"It really is," said Nadia.

"I was just asking Avery," Laurie went on. "If the two of you have figured out what's next for work?"

"Oh, I don't know," said Nadia. "We've been doing some work with Avery's family company to purchase a building in the Loop."

"Wow," said Laurie. "That sounds like a big deal."

"It's the company's first building in Chicago," said Avery. "And the deal is almost finalized." She turned momentarily from the conversation and plucked out a wine glass for Nadia, filled it, and then handed it over to her. Nadia took a sip right away.

"That sounds promising," Laurie said. "Is that something you two can make full-time?"

Nadia and Avery looked to one another knowingly.

"I think the situation is a bit complicated," said Nadia. "There are some feelings involved."

Laurie raised her eyebrows, like the answer didn't make sense.

"It's a personal thing," Avery said with a sigh. "With my family. I'm not so sure I could return to working with them."

"Why not?" said Laurie. "I would love to work with my family."

"My family relationships are complex," said Avery. "We want different things."

"Avery's goal is to be CEO of a large company," said Nadia, butting in and taking charge. "But that's not possible for her at her family's company."

"Nadia, I—" protested Avery, but she immediately stopped herself and gave in. "She's right. I have my dreams and I will not achieve them at M. M. Wool Properties."

"But you enjoy working with your family?" asked Laurie.

"I do," said Avery. "We butt heads occasionally, like any family, but I do enjoy working with them."

"But your dreams are important?" Laurie said.

"They are," said Avery. "Certainly."

"I don't know," said Laurie. "Some things are worth changing your dreams for. You can't really have it all. You've got to figure out what concessions you're willing to make for the things you really want. I mean, what's the most important stuff in life? Is it career? Is it money? Is it love? Family? Anybody who thinks they can do it all is going to be really upset when they find out it never works out like that."

"What do you mean?" Nadia said with renewed interest.

"If you chase career hard and really try to get to the top," said Laurie. "You might find your love life really suffers. Or if you try to pile up as much money as you can, you might do so while unknowingly neglecting your family. I'm just trying to say, you can't have it all. You have to choose."

Avery took a slow drink from her glass and remained silent. Laurie's words strangely resonated with her. For as long as she could remember, having it all had been her goal. But it was only when she took a step back, agreeing to come to Chicago, that she had met Nadia. And now that she had stepped back yet again from work, her relationship with Nadia had gotten even better.

"That makes sense," said Nadia. "This Color Wheel thing taught me a valuable lesson about my work life and I don't think it's one I'll soon forget."

"Even something you've worked really hard at can be taken away," said Laurie. "Life is a total crapshoot in that way."

"Are you all right?" Nadia asked Avery, who's eyes had glazed over. She gave Avery a light nudge.

"Hmm?" intoned Avery. "Oh. Yes, I am fine." She offered a simple smile. "You know, I really enjoy the roof on your building. Would you ladies like to go upstairs?"

"I'm down," said Laurie, taking the last sip in her glass. "Let's bring a couple of bottles."

"Yep," said Nadia, corking the open bottle of wine and picking it up. Laurie then grabbed one of the unopened bottles and the corkscrew.

Nadia and Laurie prepared to leave, but Avery lingered, still in a bit of a daze.

"You coming?" Nadia asked her, as Laurie opened up the door.

"Yes," Avery said, smiling and returning to the conversation. "Yes, I'm right behind you."

AVERY SAT CROSSLEGGED on the couch, wearing a silk

camisole and matching underwear, with her laptop resting on her thighs as she typed quickly into the keyboard. She was finishing up an email, and after she read it over twice, she hit send and sighed audibly. Tomorrow her work with the building purchase would come to an end, as the contracts were to be signed and M. M. Wool would take possession. It felt good to bring this purchase to completion. It felt like old times. And just like old times, she was exhausted from the process.

She shut her laptop and tossed it to the couch. The lights were low in the living room, as Nadia had already gone to bed about an hour before. Avery rubbed her eyes and looked around. She found herself wishing that Nadia was still up. Despite that it was getting late, finishing a project always gave Avery a sense of wanting more. It was a blessing and a curse. She was never satisfied, always ready for the next challenge. It was something she had to work on, she knew. But it was who she was.

Standing up from the couch, Avery put her hands above her head and stretched, her top pulling upwards slightly as she did. She then plucked her empty water glass from the coffee table and walked it into the kitchen. It was quiet in the loft condo. Avery looked around the place once again, and a smile came to her lips. This wasn't the kind of place she had imagined she would end up when she came to Chicago, but it was a welcome surprise. And her growing feelings for Nadia were a welcome surprise as well.

Avery slowly ambled toward the bedroom and she looked inside. There, sleeping on her stomach, was Nadia.

The sheet barely covered her, and Avery could see that Nadia was only wearing underwear and no top. The summer had been growing in temperature, and Nadia liked to sleep with the window open. Faint city sounds came in through the window, not loud enough to disturb sleep but just low enough to lull you into your dreams.

Stepping closer to bed, Avery smiled to herself as she admired Nadia. She was a beautiful woman, young and smart, driven and serious when she had to be, but she also had a goofy side. Avery delighted in Nadia's charms. They made her feel young again. Not that she necessarily felt old, but she had dedicated so much of her time to rising in business, it often struck her how quickly the time went. Avery sat down on the bed next to Nadia and slowly began caressing her rear, her hand gliding smoothly over the elastic fabric of Nadia's panties.

Nadia stirred where she slept, her legs pumping slightly, and then she turned over slowly, exposing her bare chest, and opened her eyes. When she noticed Avery looking down at her, a sleepy smile moved over her lips.

"Hi," said Nadia in a low voice.

"Hi," said Avery.

"Did you finish your work?"

"I did."

"Well, come to bed," said Nadia. She lazily stretched out in the sheets, her arms raising up into the pillows.

"How would you expect me to sleep when you're looking so sexy lying there," said Avery. She put her hands on Nadia's stomach and slowly moved them upwards toward Nadia's breasts.

"Oh, is that what you want?" said Nadia, watching Avery's hands. Just as they were about to grope Nadia's chest, Avery changed directions and slowly dragged them back down over Nadia's stomach. Nadia felt herself shiver in anticipation.

Avery then brought her hands down to Nadia's underwear, and she pinched at the waistband, giving it a teasing pull up off of Nadia's body. Nadia watched and smiled and let Avery have her way. Her arousal mounted and she was eager for the attention.

"I could just pull these down a little bit," mused Avery, pulling Nadia's panties down now ever so slightly, exposing Nadia's dark bush. With one hand, Avery held the elastic fabric down, while her other pet through Nadia's fur.

"Mmm," hummed Nadia. "That feels nice."

"What's down here?" teased Avery. She slipped a single finger down the length of Nadia's slit, parting her soft lips and feeling the slightest bit of tacky wetness. Avery moved her finger back and forth, until she settled it on Nadia's clit. She began to slowly rub in small circles.

"Oh God," said Nadia, giving a half-laugh and twisting a bit where she lay. "There it is." She then reached down and pawed at her underwear, trying to push at them. "Take these off of me."

"With pleasure," said Avery. With her free hand, she deftly pulled Nadia's underwear down, guiding them over her thighs, all while keeping her other hand pressed to

Nadia's middle, tenderly massaging her clit. As Nadia's panties neared her feet, she kicked them off.

"Now I can spread out," said Nadia, widening her legs and opening herself up to lust. Avery grinned, looking down into Nadia's beckoning love.

As Avery lowered herself and dove in, Nadia tossed her head back and closed her eyes. She could feel Avery's tongue exploring her, running up the length of her slit, kissing and sucking at her wet flesh. Her body ached with desire, and thoughts of passion filled her mind. Nadia quickly opened her eyes and looked down the moment she felt Avery reach up and grab at her tit, offering it a firm squeeze, all while her mouth remained attached to Nadia's pussy. Nadia couldn't help but release a long moan, drop her head back down, and succumb to the quickly growing intensity inside of her.

In the bedroom, Nadia and Avery always felt perfectly in sync. Their lovemaking was just natural, easy, effortless. And Avery's confidence brought out a confidence in Nadia that she had never known before. She was never embarrassed to try things out or take chances. Avery opened something up within that she had never known. It was an unbridled lust that made Nadia feel like an entirely new woman.

And when Nadia came, it was always an event. Her body shivered and vibrated with a fervent zeal, orgasmic release that she had only sporadically experienced in the past. But with Avery, it felt like every time they made love Nadia discovered a new part of her body that could tingle like never before. It was bliss.

Later, as they were laying in bed in a post-sex collapse, both women naked and sweaty, Nadia hung on to Avery with her hand idly petting over Avery's trimmed blonde bush. The short hairs tickled Nadia's hand and she loved the feeling of it on her palm. Avery's flesh was lightly tacky, a hint of wetness still lingering. Occasionally, Nadia lowered her finger and traced it lightly up and down her lover's slit, feeling her lips casually part.

"Mmm," intoned Avery with exhausted joy on her face.

"I love doing that with you," Nadia mused, kissing the side of Avery's head. "It makes me feel wonderful."

"We should do it again," said Avery.

"Isn't it getting late?"

"Who cares?"

Nadia laughed softly and kissed Avery once more.

"Thank you for showing yourself to me," said Nadia. "I really adore this side of you."

"Oh?" Avery said, lifting an eyebrow.

"You know, you put up a good front and all that," Nadia continued. "But I know who you really are."

"A maniac," said Avery. "I'm a maniac." Nadia laughed again.

"Maybe," said Nadia. "But you're a caring and attentive woman. You take what you want, but you also love to give it, too."

"That's true," Avery admitted. "There's certainly a bedroom Avery that goes along with boardroom Avery. And sometimes they meet in the middle."

"I don't care about anything that happens outside of

this," said Nadia, rolling over and tossing a leg over Avery's leg, positioning herself halfway on top of her. "This is all I need." She leaned down and delicately pressed her lips to Avery's.

"I'm really beginning to feel the same," said Avery. "And that's very new for me." Nadia grinned happily and instigated another kiss.

Before long, the two women were lovingly cuddled up together, limbs intertwined, dozing toward sleep as their bodies relaxed and eased into the soft bed. A cool breeze came in through the open window, and Avery pulled at the sheet to cover them both. She looked at Nadia, who was now asleep, and Avery smiled. She kissed Nadia's cheek, and then she closed her eyes and laid her head next to Nadia's on the pillow.

"IT HAS BEEN a pleasure doing business with you," said Charles, standing up from his chair and extending his hand to another man about his age. They had just signed the contracts for the purchase of the building, M. M. Wool's first in Chicago, and there was a sense of relief in the meeting room. Nadia and Avery stood off to the side, watching with smiles on their faces as the sale was finalized.

"Indeed," said the man as he shook Charles' hand. "We wish you luck with this endeavor. It is a fine market and you should do well."

"Thank you," said Charles, bowing his head slightly.

Nadia had never been witness to such a large financial transaction. There were executives from both companies present, lawyers, accountants, insurance people, and a host of others that she wasn't quite sure about. The wildest part, to Nadia at least, was that nobody in the room appeared too moved. That is, swapping a building in downtown Chicago for an extraordinarily large amount of money appeared to be quite common for all those involved. Not even Avery seemed to flinch.

It was an eye-opening experience. It reminded Nadia of when she bought her condo. Only this was, of course, a much bigger deal.

As the group of people around the conference table stood up, congratulations all around, and they all started to collect their things and move toward the exit, Nadia looked to Avery with a big grin on her face and wide eyes.

"I can't believe I just watched eighty-six million dollars change hands," Nadia said in a whisper. "It really blows my mind." Avery returned Nadia's smile.

"It's surely a lot of money," said Avery. "But it's certainly not the largest deal we've ever made. Buildings in New York City are far more expensive."

"Oh, I'm sure," replied Nadia. "But I can hardly fathom what this amount of money looks like. I was imagining it being brought to the table in a suitcase. Or, well, *many* suit-cases." Avery laughed.

"Yes, wouldn't that be something," she said. "Woe are we that it all comes down to a simple wire transfer."

Just then, Charles walked up to where Nadia and Avery

stood. He was in a suit, and his hair was immaculately trimmed and styled. He offered the women an affable smile.

"Ladies," he said as he approached. "I just wanted to offer my sincerest gratitude for your efforts in making this deal happen. It was quite convenient for us to have you here for the various inspections and meetings and such during the process. There was no way that Max or I could fly out for each of those."

"You're quite welcome, Dad," Avery said and smiled. "It felt just like old times for me."

"Yes," he agreed. "And Nadia, thank you as well."

"Oh, I don't really feel like I did anything at all," Nadia said, blushing slightly. "I just assisted Avery with whatever she asked. It wasn't much, really."

"Well, regardless," said Charles. "It was good to have trustworthy individuals here in Chicago during the process." His face changed from cordial to uncertain, and he looked toward Avery. "You know, Avery," he began. "It would be most preferable for M. M. Wool if we could entice you back in a greater capacity. Max and I have spoke further on the idea, and we agree that we should like you to rejoin the family business."

"I just don't know," said Avery. "You know my hesitation. I have grander dreams."

"Yes, dear, I know," Charles replied. "But you are still a young woman, and you have plenty of years left. Many people do not make CEO until later in life."

"You were CEO and president of M. M. Wool when you were my age," countered Avery.

"That was because my father died and it had become my turn," said Charles. "Regrettably. I was thrown into the fire before it was truly my time. I hope to not do that to you and Max."

"Still," said Avery. "I know where you stand with passing the company down when it's time. And while I understand your reasoning, I do hope one day to be the chief executive. Somewhere."

"Had you went to law school," said Charles. "We might be having a different conversation."

The way Avery and Charles spoke to one another felt very formal to Nadia. They were from a completely different world. It wasn't that there was a lack of love between the Wool family, they just operated in a very courtly manner. It was almost as though their conversations were always a debate of logic. Nadia's family was far more relaxed and animated than what she saw between Avery and her family.

"I understand," said Avery. "But I do have an MBA and I am very worthy."

"That you are," said Charles. "Returning to my point, however. Max and I would be very interested in offering you — *both* of you," he said, looking to Nadia for a moment. "A position with the company in regards to our expanding business here in Chicago."

"A job?" blurted out Nadia. "Sir, I'm not even sure what I have to offer M. M. Wool."

"She has a lot to offer," Avery butted in, offering Nadia a glance. "Nadia's expertise in advertising and working with clients directly could certainly help us with tenant placement and retention."

"Agreed," said Charles. "And Avery, if you return to the company there will be an executive position waiting for you, though we would prefer that you stay in Chicago for the time being as we grow our portfolio in this market."

"I think this is something that Nadia and I will have to talk over," Avery said. "Neither of us would want to be impetuous in this decision."

"I believe that's smart," said Charles. "Well, please consider it and let me know when you've decided one way or another." He smiled easily, and he moved his eyes to Nadia. "Again, Nadia, thank you very much for your help."

"You're welcome, Mr. Wool," said Nadia.

"And Avery," said Charles. He leaned in and kissed her on the cheek. "We will be in contact. Thank you for your help. Max and I will be heading back to New York this afternoon."

"Have a good flight, Dad," said Avery, her smile slowly growing.

"Yes, thank you," Charles said. He bowed his head at the women and then stepped away.

Once Nadia and Avery were outside of the meeting room and walking down the hallway toward an office they had set up in, Nadia couldn't hold in her surprise any longer.

"Your father really wants to offer me a job," she said. "Avery, I have no experience whatsoever in real estate. That's crazy."

"You have some experience now," Avery said and grinned.

"Barely," Nadia replied. "All I really did was make some calls for you and set up meetings with contractors. It wasn't much different than what I was doing at Color Wheel. Coordinating with people to make things happen."

"Exactly," said Avery. "At a certain level, that's what the work entails. It's management. You can do that, whether it's for an advertising agency or a real estate investment company."

"What would it involve?" asked Nadia, as the two of them walked into the office. Their laptops were both sitting closed on the desk, along with a few folders of paper. They began cleaning up and preparing to leave.

"The job?" said Avery.

"Yes."

"M. M. Wool, when buying a new property, installs their own management office in the building," said Avery. "We deal with tenants, with the engineers, with every little thing that helps a building function. I imagine my father would want me to run this office for a time, and you would be my assistant." Avery smiled simply.

"Are you going to do it?" Nadia said. Her face conveyed bewilderment, like this was happening very fast.

"I have to think about it a little more," said Avery. She paused and then she sighed. "What my father said really makes sense."

"What's that?" said Nadia.

"There's still plenty of time for me to achieve my

dreams," she replied. "It doesn't have to happen today or tomorrow or even next week. Getting what I truly want out of life is a long climb. I've had a setback, but returning to my family's business could reposition me for something greater in the future."

"Your father seems like a very smart man," said Nadia. "He really commands respect."

"Truly," Avery agreed. "I feel like maybe I've been rebelling somewhat in regards to him. But he's always wanted what's best for me. And never once has he held a grudge against me, not even when I left M. M. Wool for Scheffler & Vonn. He kissed me and wished me luck."

Nadia smiled and lifted her bag up on to her shoulder. After a silence, she stepped closer to Avery and she kissed her tenderly on the lips.

A sense of calm and happiness moved over Avery's face with that kiss. And once the two were ready, they made their exit from the office, both with a lot of new things to consider. Being together, however, made those considerations just that much easier.

NADIA WALKED into the coffee shop, holding her bag against her side, and she looked around to see if she had arrived first. After a moment, she smiled when she spotted Frances. Frances noticed Nadia as well, she smiled big, and she waved Nadia over to the table where she was sitting. Almost bounding over, Nadia felt undeniably happy to see her old boss. And when she arrived at the table, Frances stood up, and the two women hugged.

"It's so great to see you, Nadia," said Frances, stepping back from the hug. "You look well."

"Thank you," Nadia replied with a smile. "It's great to see you, too."

"I got you a coffee," Frances said, motioning with her hand to the cup sitting on the table.

"Perfect," said Nadia. As the two women sat down in their seats, Nadia went for the coffee and took a small sip of the hot liquid. She then blew on it.

"Might still be rather hot," noted Frances.

"I see that," Nadia said. She laughed and sat upright in her chair. "Thank you so much for meeting me here, Frances. I'm glad I caught you before you moved away."

"We're very close to selling the house," Frances said, "Then we're going on a trip, as all of our things get moved out to Colorado."

"That all sounds like an exciting adventure," Nadia said happily.

"Oh, it will be," Frances assured her. "And after all these years of working, I am ready for some adventure."

"You know," Nadia started. "I called you here to talk a little bit about work... and life."

"Nadia, dear," said Frances. "I'm sorry about how things worked out with Color Wheel. That wasn't how I wanted it to go down. I tried to protect you all in the buy-out, but Scheffler & Vonn are just vultures. There wasn't much else I could do."

"No, I understand," said Nadia. "It's been an adjustment process. But I'm past it. I can't get angry about something that was so far out of my control."

"I'm glad to hear it," said Frances. "Though I'm sure it's quite easy to be mad at that Avery Wool," she said, shaking her head. "She definitely pulled the wool over our eyes."

"No," countered Nadia simply. "I'm not mad at Avery. I'm dating her, actually."

"You're *dating* her?" Frances repeated incredulously with a laugh. "Isn't that something?"

"It's been a wild ride," said Nadia. "That's for certain. No, Avery also lost her job. Shipping her out to Color Wheel was their way of getting rid of her."

"*Really?*" said Frances. "Wow. These big corporations, they really will eat their own. It's rather ironic, isn't it?"

"Definitely," said Nadia. She smiled and tried her coffee once more. It had begun to cool.

"Well, things have a tendency to work out strangely," said Frances. "Never did I even imagine that Color Wheel would become what it did. And never would I have imagined I'd sell out for so much money to such a big company. Moving to Colorado, that was always a dream of mine and now it's about to become a reality."

"Things do work out strangely," mused Nadia. "And that's sort of why I asked to meet with you."

"Oh?" Frances asked, lifting a brow and taking a drink of her coffee.

"Things are going really well with Avery," said Nadia with confidence. "I really like her."

"Her?" asked Frances skeptically. "She's a pretty stoic woman."

"Yes, she can be," said Nadia. "But having gotten to know her better, I can see the difference between her business facade and her heart. She's definitely complicated, but... but I really love that about her." Frances smiled and nodded.

"In business, you often have to put up some great defenses if you want to succeed," said Frances. "It can be very scary at times."

"Yes," said Nadia. "Well, speaking of business... I have a new opportunity and I was hoping to get your opinion."

"Of course," said Frances. "I'm all ears, dear."

"Well, I have this opportunity for a new job," said Nadia. "I have a few, actually."

"That's a very good position to be in."

"It is," Nadia agreed. "One, Polly offered to find me something with them out in California. Harold was always very impressed with my work, and he's sure that I could get a job working directly with them."

"That's terrific," said Frances. "That is a very good opportunity."

"It would be working in a similar capacity as I did with them at Color Wheel," said Nadia. "But on the other side of things. I mean, it does sound right up my alley, but..."

"But?"

"But I really don't want to move to California," said Nadia. "My life is here. I love Chicago, and this is where I want to be."

"Okay," said Frances. "So tell me the other opportunity."

"The other," Nadia started. "Is working with Avery. With her and her family. You see, her father has been trying to lure her back to the family business and recently she and I assisted with a building purchase for their real estate investment company. He's offered me a position."

"This is an embarrassment of riches, Nadia," said Frances. "I would say you're a very lucky woman, but I don't believe luck has anything to do with it. You're a hard worker, very bright and knowledgable, and any company that hires you on is going to be better for it."

"Thank you," Nadia said with slight embarrassment. "I appreciate that, Frances."

"It's true."

"My issue with the Wool Properties offer is…" Nadia said, trailing off as she tried to gather her thoughts. "It's just that it's so different than anything I've ever done before and I'm not totally confident that it will be a right fit. I don't want to lose this thing with Polly in California, which is totally in line with my career path, if this opportunity working for Avery's family doesn't work out. I don't know anything about real estate. I'm a graphic designer and a marketer, you know?"

"You know that I was a high school teacher at one time," said Frances in a serious tone. "Here in Chicago, I taught art and English. But unfortunately, teaching jobs in Chicago aren't a very secure thing and I was laid off after a few years of doing it. I was pulling my hair out, Nadia, I was wrecked.

I had studied a long time to be a teacher, it was what I had always wanted to do."

"I don't know if I knew that about you," Nadia mused.

"I mean, I had *really* always wanted to be an artist," said Frances. "But everybody *knows* you can't make any money like that." She laughed. "Or so we're all told. A friend of mine said to me, she said, 'Frances, you're a young woman with so much time ahead of you. Just try it. Just try to be an artist, to do your design work. If it fails, you can always find another teaching job." Frances smiled to herself and she took a drink.

"You never did get another teaching job," said Nadia knowingly.

"I did not," said Frances. "No. I took a shot on something I had no idea about. I had taken a few design courses in college, but never with the intention of being a designer myself. And never did I think my small freelance design business would turn into what it did. Although some days I do lament that it's gone, I can't help but believe that my risks and all my hard work paid off. Look at me now. I'm retired. I have more money than I will ever be able to spend. And I'm free to live my life how I see fit. All because I took a shot. You get what I'm saying, Nadia?"

"I think I do," said Nadia, slowly nodding.

"And besides," Frances continued. "I've told you over and over again. You're a smart cookie. You're talented at what you do. Our clients always loved working with you, and so did the other employees. You are destined to succeed if you just keep up what you're doing. Advertising, real estate, I don't think it matters. I think that you're going to be successful in whatever it is you decide to do."

"That feels so good to hear you say," Nadia replied with a reassured smile. "It means a lot coming from you. You've always been a mentor to me."

"And the worst case scenario," said Frances. "If it doesn't work out, you've got a hell of a portfolio and I highly doubt you'll ever have difficulty getting a job in advertising. You know you can always get a letter of recommendation out of me."

"I sincerely appreciate that, Frances," said Nadia. She reached across the table and squeezed Frances' hand. Frances grinned and returned the squeeze.

"Now listen," said Frances. "You've got to tell me this story about you and Avery getting together. I really had no idea."

Nadia laughed and nodded. It was pretty ridiculous.

"All right," said Nadia, smiling warmly across the table at her boss, her friend, her mentor. "It's definitely been an interesting trip..."

THE SUN WAS SETTING and Nadia pushed her sunglasses up onto her head, as they were no longer needed. She was sitting at the picnic table up on her building's roof, with her notebook in front of her and a pen in her hand. Scribbling her thoughts down onto the page, Nadia weighed the options in front of her. There was a lot to consider, and she always found it easier to make decisions when she wrote out all the pros and cons.

Looking out at the Chicago city skyline, a smile came to her lips. She couldn't leave this town. It was all she had known, the place where she grew up, and it held a firm place in her heart. California didn't call to her like it might to some others. No, this was where she wanted to be. Despite the offer from Polly, it was never really a choice she was willing to make. Chicago was home.

But it was a far more difficult decision to leave the business she had always thought of as her career. When you write a narrative for yourself over the years, it's not so easy to change the definitions of who you are or what you want to be. Sometimes, though, life can show you that you're not as in control as you once thought you were. The story you have written for yourself is just that — it's a story, and it doesn't always flow with what fate has waiting for you.

Nadia set her pen down just as she heard the door to the roof open. Looking toward the door, she saw Avery and Laurie walking through it. They were laughing, and they each held a bottle of wine and glasses. It put a smile on Nadia's face that the two of them were getting along. Laurie had had some unkind things to say about Avery over the preceding months, but she had come to learn, just as Nadia had, that Avery had just been a pawn in a corporate game. Avery knew that, too, and it had very noticeably changed her. As the two women approached the picnic table, they both smiled and held their wine bottles aloft.

"Special delivery!" said Laurie. She laughed and set the

bottle on the table, along with her glass. Avery followed suit, putting one glass down near herself and one in front of Nadia.

"You ladies read my mind," said Nadia.

"Laurie was just telling me that her *new* company is going through a buy-out now as well," said Avery. "Isn't that absurd?"

"You're kidding me," said Nadia, looking up to Laurie. "When does it ever end?"

"Yeah, it's some sick joke," Laurie replied, laughing and shaking her head. She threw a leg over the table bench and sat opposite Nadia. "I can't even let it get me down. It's just too funny."

"I'm not sure I'd call it *funny*," countered Nadia.

"I'm hopeful, though," said Laurie. "I've heard that the company has actually changed hands a few times."

"Are you enjoying it there?" Avery asked, sitting next to Nadia now. She dropped her hand underneath the table and rested it on Nadia's bare thigh.

"At Digimedia?" said Laurie. "Yeah, I am. It's a bit more corporate than Color Wheel was, unfortunately. You know, very bureaucratic. But I've been getting on with my coworkers well, my salary is better. It's fine for now."

"I've definitely decided," said Nadia firmly. "I'm not going to pursue the job with Polly. I just can't see myself moving to California, as good as a job as it could be." Avery smiled happily and rubbed Nadia's leg.

"I knew that all along," said Laurie, taking a drink from

her glass. "I knew there was no way you'd leave this city, as much as you hemmed and hawed about it."

"I don't think I hemmed and hawed all that much," protested Nadia. Laurie laughed and shrugged.

"I've been thinking about our options as well," said Avery. "And I spoke to my father. I've decided to return to M. M. Wool and resume my position there."

"Yeah?" said Nadia, smiling and looking at Avery. "Does that mean you're going to stay in Chicago?"

"For the foreseeable future," said Avery, returning the smile. "Yes, I am staying in Chicago."

Nadia grinned and she leaned closer to Avery, pushing a grateful kiss on her lover's lips.

"I may not like certain things about working with my family," Avery continued. "But they are still my family and I still have a lot of years left in me to achieve my dreams. We all tend to glorify youth, and think that if we don't achieve the greatness we desire at a young age then we will never achieve it. But patience is a virtue, I believe, and I will get to where I want to go eventually. For now, I am content with how things are." She kissed Nadia once more.

"What about you, Nadia?" asked Laurie. "What are you thinking?"

"I'm still not completely sure," said Nadia. She patted her notebook. "I've been making lists and really thinking hard about it, but I'm not sure if I want to continue down the path I've been on for my entire adult life, or if I'm ready to change gears and try something else. It's scary, you know?"

"Nadia, you are so talented," said Laurie. "You will thrive with whatever you do."

Avery just smiled in agreement, nodding her head along with Laurie's words.

"I think it's more like... I've invested so much of myself in this narrow field," said Nadia. "It's hard to let go. I guess I've sort of defined myself as a designer and advertising professional for so long, it's tough to see myself as anything other than that."

"I feel the same way," said Avery. "But for me, everything I have done was a calculation to get me to the coveted top executive position. I could almost taste it when I was running Color Wheel for that short time. It's hard to redefine your life, but sometimes it's what we have to do if we want to be happy."

"I am happy," said Nadia. She threaded her fingers into Avery's, and they both squeezed.

"And so am I," agreed Avery with a smile.

The evening continued on, and as the sun finally set and the moon appeared, the three women continued their conversation amid candle light. They were laughing and having fun, mostly through their second bottle of wine and feeling buzzed. It was a relaxed late summer night, warm yet comfortable, with easy conversation among friends. Avery had worked herself seamlessly in since moving into Nadia's condo, and it made Nadia feel quite content to know that her girlfriend and her best friend had begun forging a friendship of their own.

After a while longer, Laurie excused herself for the night

as she had some chores to finish. And once she left the roof, the tempo changed. Nadia casually laid her head on Avery's shoulder and she released a happy sigh. Everything felt perfect in that moment. Everything felt easy and free.

"I really do think you should come work with me," said Avery to break the silence.

"I don't know if I'm ready to make a decision yet," Nadia replied.

"What about your conversation with Frances?" Avery said. "She had some very convincing things to say."

"That's true," said Nadia. "I just have some more thinking to do."

"Do what's best for you," said Avery. "I will happily accept your decision either way."

"Thank you," said Nadia, smiling and closing her eyes. She cuddled up against Avery, wrapping her arms around her lover's waist. Avery, too, smiled and eased into the embrace. She felt like a transformed woman. The life she had been living for so long felt as though it was beginning to fade away into something far better. This was enough. What she had with Nadia, the prospect of returning to the family business, it was all she really needed to be happy.

"I used to think that the purpose of life was to achieve greater and greater things, "Avery said after some time in silence. "Nothing was ever good enough, more was always better, once I reached a higher platform my eyes immediately went to the next step."

"The American way," Nadia responded with a light laugh. Avery chuckled as well.

"Yes," she agreed. "But I just don't know anymore. With each greater step I've taken, it really hasn't brought me greater happiness. Since dialing it back, however, since falling from my position, losing what I have been building, I think I've received a much more important lesson than whatever it was that I've lost," said Avery. "There is more to life than achievement."

"And what's that?" Nadia asked.

"There's *this*," said Avery. "Sitting up on this roof with your partner, your lover, not thinking about work or business or whatever else might preoccupy the mind of an over-achiever. Nadia, I am beginning to find true happiness. And it feels far different than I expected it to."

"What do you mean?" said Nadia. "What's the difference?"

"I thought I would find real happiness in sitting in a big leather chair behind a desk," said Avery. "Steering a giant corporate ship. But the way I feel right this moment, compared to my brushes with that... well, it doesn't even compare. I'm feeling much more content just *being* than I did when I was constantly pushing."

Nadia smiled, head still on Avery's shoulder. She turned her head and kissed Avery's neck lightly, giving Avery a slight tickle. She squirmed and she laughed.

"Let's go downstairs," Nadia said in a low tone. "I want to make love to you."

"I thought you'd never ask," Avery replied with a sly, excited grin.

NADIA PUSHED herself up from the floor, her head down, her rear up, arms and legs going as straight as they could. She, along with a class of about ten other people, were moving into downward dog, sweaty hands gripping to the yoga mats below. At the front of the class, the teacher, a young slim woman who looked like she did nothing but yoga, demonstrated the perfect form and called out in a firm but calm voice the next pose they would be doing. Nadia's arms shook slightly as she lowered herself completely flat down onto the mat in unison with the rest of the students.

It had been over a month since her time at Color Wheel came to an end and she didn't find herself missing work at all. The severance that Avery had made sure she got was enough to comfortably float her for a while, and she was enjoying the first time off of working she had had since college. Avery, on the other hand — and despite her declarations that she was cured from being a workaholic — was already back to work with her family's real estate company. Nadia knew she couldn't avoid work, or avoid making a decision on what to do next, for much longer, but being able to take yoga class in the middle of the morning on a weekday was definitely a perk of being unemployed.

But she was dating a very wealthy woman who couldn't tear herself away from business. Nadia didn't want to take advantage of the relationship, but it also made her feel a renewed sense of freedom and possibility in her life. It made her feel for the very first time like she had a bit of leeway to figure out what she truly wanted to do with herself.

Her dark hair back in a ponytail, her cheeks slightly rosy from exertion, Nadia tucked her rolled up yoga mat under her arm as the class concluded. She looked around the studio at all the fit, healthy people — mostly woman, and one man — and pondered how it was that they were able to attend a yoga class with such leisure. Where they in similar situations as she was? Between jobs, but with some savings to give them some time to figure it all out? Or maybe they were all attached to a wealthy partner as well.

Nadia couldn't help herself, as her curiosity was just too much. She picked one of the students, a blonde woman who looked to be in her mid-thirties like Nadia, and she casually ambled up next to her as she rolled her mat. Nadia pretended like she had something to do near the woman, like she was looking for something, before finally opening her mouth to speak.

"That was a good class," Nadia said. The woman, who was squatting down with her completely rolled up mat, looked up to Nadia and smiled. She stood up.

"Janie is great," said the woman, referring to the teacher. "She's so young, but she's been doing yoga forever and she's such a wonderful teacher."

"How young is she?" Nadia asked.

"Um, she's twenty-three, I think," said the woman. "But she's been seriously doing yoga since she was ten. Isn't that unbelievable?"

"Wow, yeah," agreed Nadia. "That's crazy."

"I've only been at it for five," said the woman. She paused, smiled, and then stuck out her hand. "I'm Ellen."

"Nadia," she replied, shaking Ellen's hand. "It's nice to meet you."

"You too," said Ellen. "I've seen you a few times recently in this class."

"I only just started coming," said Nadia. "I've got some free time lately and I figured I should finally get back into yoga. I've done it off and on, more in college than I've been able to do in the last few years."

"I got into it after I had my daughter," said Ellen. "It was really just a way to get back in shape after the pregnancy, but I fell in love with it. I'm going to enroll in teacher training."

"Teacher training?" said Nadia.

"Yeah," said Ellen. "The studio offers an intensive course over three months. Then you can become a certified yoga teacher."

"That's really interesting," mused Nadia. "I hadn't thought of that."

"I'm excited," said Ellen. "Hey. Do you want to come with me to the juice bar a few doors down? I always get a green juice after class."

"Sure," Nadia replied with a growing smile. "I'd like that."

The women sat together at a small table in the juice bar, their yoga mats propped up against the wall. The sunlight from outside shone in through the large windows at the storefront. Everything was bright and clean inside the juice bar, and a steady stream of patrons walked in, lined up, ordered their drink, and filtered out. Nadia raised her clear cup up and slowly sipped the green liquid through the straw. It had a subtle sweetness to it, but also a bitterness. It was good.

"Right now," said Ellen. "I try to come to class three days a week. But once teacher training starts, I'm going to be at the studio every day."

"That sounds pretty intense," said Nadia. "But it also sounds kind of dreamy."

"It's perfect for me," said Ellen. "I drop my daughter off at school in the morning, then I can come to yoga, then run any errands, and then she's ready to be picked up. I mean, she's just a few blocks away. I rarely have to even leave the neighborhood."

"I've had a pretty open schedule since I lost my job," Nadia admitted. Ellen made an empathetic face.

"Aw, I'm sorry," she said. "That's unfortunate."

"It's not bad, really," said Nadia. "I really liked it, but the company got bought out and then eventually shut down. But now that I'm out of that world, I feel a lot lighter."

"After raising a kid," said Ellen. "Some days I *miss* the office." She laughed and Nadia smiled.

"I have some options, some other offers," said Nadia. "But none of them really get me going. I just don't feel really passionate about any of the decisions."

"What did you do?" asked Ellen.

"I worked in advertising," said Nadia.

"That's what I did!" Ellen quickly replied, eyes brightening up. "I did copywriting. But I left when Meredith was born. My husband does pretty well for us, so it's more important that I'm around to raise her."

"Now that I'm a bit removed from it all," Nadia said. "I don't really miss the advertising world."

"I know, right?" said Ellen. "It can be a drag. You're just pushing products you don't really care about. Trying to convince people to buy things. Sometimes I didn't feel too great about doing that."

"I started in graphic design," said Nadia. "Which I really loved. But eventually I was in a management role and, even though I was good at it, it was just starting to feel like it was a big departure from what I originally wanted."

"Well, it seems like you've got some time to figure out what's next," Ellen said with a smile. She put her lips around her straw and drank her juice.

"I do," said Nadia. "Maybe I'll be a yoga teacher." She smiled and shrugged.

"You could!" said Ellen enthusiastically. "Why not?"

"Yoga teachers don't make very much money, do they?" Nadia asked.

"Well, no," said Ellen. "But if you got a following, if you taught at a few studios, you never know what might happen."

"Is that your plan?" Nadia said.

"No," Ellen replied. "I mean, we're doing okay. I'm just doing it to take yoga bit more seriously and stay in shape. I will try to pick up a class or two once I'm certified, but I don't plan to really pursue a career with it."

"But a career *is* possible, isn't it?" Nadia pressed.

"I *think*," said Ellen. "I guess you might have to ask some of the teachers at the studio what they think. If they're doing it, it must be possible."

"Maybe I will," Nadia said, looking off in the distance as she pondered the possibility. It wasn't something she had ever considered, but it did sound like it could be fun and fulfilling. She had enjoyed being in yoga class, and the thought of doing it more frequently was enticing.

"Ooh," intoned Ellen, looking at her phone. "Nadia, I've got to jet." Ellen pushed back from the table and stood up. "I still need to hit the grocery store. But it was really nice talking to you."

"It was nice talking to you, too," Nadia replied, smiling contentedly up at her new friend.

"And I'll see you in class again, right?" asked Ellen. "Will you be there in the next few days?"

"Definitely," said Nadia. "I'll definitely be back."

"Great," said Ellen. "Maybe we can get a juice again, as well."

"I'd like that," said Nadia.

Ellen picked up her things and exchanged a few more pleasantries with Nadia, before saying a cheerful goodbye and making her way toward the exit. Nadia watched Ellen go, smiling to herself, and feeling pretty good about making a new connection with someone in her neighborhood. She was glad she had decided to speak to Ellen after class, and their conversation had given her something completely novel to ponder over.

As she casually continued to drink her juice alone, Nadia wondered what Avery might think about it all.

AVERY SAT IN HER OFFICE, leaning back in her desk chair, holding the phone up to her ear. She rocked back and forth lightly, staring into her computer screen, while the voice on the other end — her father's voice — ran through some of the issues that they were currently dealing with. Avery had a serious and focused look on her face.

"Alex from the IT department will be flying out there next week," said Charles. "While I'm not sure the extent of his trip, I do know he will be establishing some link between Chicago and our offices here in New York."

"That's fine," replied Avery.

"We want you to have access to our shared data folders," Charles continued. "Are there any pressing needs on your end as far as IT is concerned?"

"I would like a computer for the as-of-yet un-hired assistant manager's office," said Avery. "I want to be prepared for when I make that hire."

"Yes," said Charles. "And no word from Nadia on whether or not she would accept such a position?"

"She's still undecided," said Avery. "I've been trying to push her in this direction, but I think that she's very much still pondering over her career."

"Understandable," said Charles. "Well, keep me posted.

I'm sure anybody you choose, whether it is Nadia or someone else, will be a good fit for the company."

"Thank you," said Avery. "Was there anything else you wanted to talk about?"

"I believe that's it," said Charles. "I am glad to have you back, Avery. While I know this isn't your ideal, I see big things for our expansion to the Chicago market and it will be very beneficial for us to have you leading the charge."

"Thank you, Dad," said Avery, a small smile curling on her lips. "And you know I do enjoy working with you. I've been reevaluating my feelings and my goals lately and I'm feeling quite content with my decision to return to the company."

"That is great to hear," he said. "You take care, dear, and we will be in touch soon."

"You too, Dad," said Avery. "Goodbye."

"Goodbye."

Avery placed her phone handset back on the receiver and sat up straight in her chair. The next item on her to-do list popped into her head, and she quickly navigated to a spreadsheet on her computer concerning tenant lease agreements. But she was soon interrupted by her young administrative assistant, a twenty-something named Elena.

"Excuse me, Avery," said Elena, popping half-way into Avery's office.

"Yes?" Avery asked.

"You have a visitor," Elena continued. "Nadia Marek."

"Nadia's here?" she replied with a smile. "Send her in. She's my girlfriend, Elena."

"Oh," Elena said, smiling and nodding. "Okay, that's good to know."

Elena exited Avery's office, and Avery heard her lightly speak in the other room. And then, in just another moment, Nadia was walking into the office with a big grin on her face.

"This place is nice," remarked Nadia, looking around and taking in Avery's office.

"It's finally finished," said Avery, moving around her desk and approaching Nadia. They embraced and they kissed.

"Has it been a strange transition for you?" asked Nadia. "Is it just you and your assistant out there?"

"Yes," Avery admitted. "Even at M. M. Wool corporate, when I worked there, the office was far more busy. This is an absolute ghost town." The women both laughed.

"I'm sure it will build up eventually," said Nadia. "This is just the beginning stages."

"My father is already talking about adding another Chicago building to the portfolio," said Avery. "So yes, it might start growing quickly."

"Wow," mused Nadia. "Already? That's quick."

"When an opportunity comes on the market," said Avery. "You have to jump at it."

"Yeah, I guess so."

"Hey," said Avery, giving Nadia a light smack on the arm. "Follow me."

"Okay," said Nadia with some confusion, but obeying Avery's orders and following her out of her office.

They didn't go very far, just to the next office over from Avery's. When they walked in, Nadia looked around and nodded as she assayed the space. It was very much like Avery's, with the same desk and desk chair, and there was a glass table off to one side with cushy leather chairs on either side of it. The windows spanned the wall and offered a great view of the Loop. Nadia smiled at Avery.

"This is a nice office," she said. "No computer, though," Nadia said as she pointed to the desk.

"It's coming," Avery said, giving Nadia a mock-annoyed look. "This could be your office."

"Yeah?" asked Nadia, giving the office another full look, seeing it now in a different light. The entire suite had been refurbished when M. M. Wool bought the building, and it was done in a sleek and modern style. It reminded Nadia a bit of Color Wheel, but it was definitely nicer and everything about it was brand new.

"I know you're probably getting tired of having me ask," said Avery. "But I did just get off the phone with my father and he was asking about you."

"He was?" said Nadia, suddenly feeling bad about being so indecisive. It just wasn't like her to be like this, but at the same time it felt like a respite she really needed. "I'm sorry, Avery. I didn't mean to hold the company back from anything."

"No, it's fine," Avery said, reassuring Nadia and delicately petting her on the shoulder. It was obvious that Avery was quite infatuated with Nadia. Avery looked at her with dreamy eyes. "I just want to make sure that you've got a good path going forward."

"You know, I've been thinking about something," admitted Nadia, leaning back against the desk, half-sitting on it, and pressing her hands into the desktop. "I didn't mention this to you yet because I wasn't sure how you'd take it."

"Okay," Avery said skeptically, standing firm and crossing her arms.

"The other day after yoga I met another student," Nadia began. "And she told me about the teacher training program at the studio."

"Teacher training?" repeated Avery. "Teaching yoga?"

"Right," said Nadia. "And I know it's out of left field, but I'm really enjoying my classes and I've just been wondering to myself... do I really belong in an office?"

"But Nadia," said Avery. "You are so good at what you do. You know that clients love you, because you are so thoughtful and attentive."

"I know," agreed Nadia. "And maybe that could be brought over to yoga. You know, I'm still not sure completely. But this really feels like a thread I might like to follow."

Avery paused for a moment and just looked at Nadia. She could tell that Nadia was being honest. There was earnestness in her expression. A slow smile came to Avery's face and she brightened up.

"Well, I think that's great," said Avery. "We can reinvent ourselves. There is no law that commands us to continue down our original path. You can always dodge through the trees and choose an entirely new path if that's what you feel is best for you."

"I appreciate that," said Nadia. She pushed herself up from where she sat on the desk and took the few steps towards Avery. Nadia embraced her tightly, and held on.

"Do you have any worries about this move?" Avery asked tenderly.

"Yes," said Nadia. "A thousand of them. But if I fail, I can always return to what I was doing before."

"Or here," said Avery. "You could always come work with me."

"That, too," Nadia said with a smile. She kissed Avery gently and then nuzzled against her cheek.

"I don't want you to worry," said Avery. "I want you to feel free to make this change without any stressors. I'm on your side," she said with love and affection in her voice, looking Nadia directly in the eyes now.

"I really appreciate that," said Nadia. "This is a very strange choice for me, but it feels like something I could really love doing."

"And I suppose it means that your flexibility will surely improve," teased Avery. Nadia laughed and nodded quickly.

"Yes, that's true," said Nadia. "I'm sure I'll eventually be able to get my legs behind my head."

"And then you're all mine," said Avery. She was grinning happily, as was Nadia. They kissed a few more times before Avery took a deep breath and stepped back. "I'm really happy things have worked out as they have. I feel like a changed woman. And honestly, I attribute much of my transformation to you."

"Really?" said Nadia. "Me? Nah."

"Yes," affirmed Avery. "Really. You've shown me a kind of love that I haven't had before. A very accepting love. And I'm grateful for that. I can be... hard-headed and over-bearing. But Nadia, you saw past that and my time here in Chicago has been truly life-changing."

"It's been really good for me, too," said Nadia, almost blushing.

"There's a few packages coming today," said Avery. "To your condo. Just some things of mine I had sent from New York. Do me a favor and don't open them before I get home tonight."

"Don't open them?" repeated Nadia with a laugh. "Secretive, huh?"

"Yes," said Avery, her eyes flashing with fiery desire. "Don't open them."

Nadia laughed once again and she nodded in acceptance. After a moment, Nadia gave in and hugged Avery yet again. She didn't want to stop. There was something even greater developing between the two, and they could both feel it.

"I love you, Avery," said Nadia as she gripped tightly. "I really do."

"And I love you, too," Avery replied, kissing Nadia on the head.

Together they stood there, holding firmly to one another. It felt as though time were standing still and that they were the only two people in existence. True love had taken hold.

NADIA CAME RUNNING into her bedroom, laughing wildly, wearing nothing but her underwear, breasts swaying as she moved, her hair flapping behind her. The room had a few comfortable orange-tinted lights on, and a hint of moonlight shined in from the windows. Behind her was Avery, she too laughing, dressed in a matching pair of sleep shorts and a camisole. Leaping onto the bed, Nadia buried her head into the pillows, as though she were hiding her face from Avery.

"You'll never get me!" called Nadia in a muffled voice.

"Oh, you bet I will!" replied Avery, she too jumping onto the bed. She straddled Nadia on her legs, pinning her down, and grabbed for her sides. Avery started to tickle Nadia and Nadia began squirming.

"No!" Nadia belted out, once more muffled by the pillows. She tried to toss Avery off of her, but it was no use. She couldn't stop laughing.

After another moment of tickling, Avery stopped and smacked Nadia on the rear. She remained sitting lightly on Nadia's thighs and started to massage her lower back, up and down. Nadia grinned to herself, still hidden among the pillows.

"That's better," Nadia said, yanking a pillow off of her head and tossing it. "I could use a massage."

"Oh yeah, you're so tense," teased Avery.

"Shut it."

"How about I open it?" asked Avery, pushing her fingers into the back of Nadia's panties and peeling them back to expose her crack. Nadia laughed again, and she reached back and swatted at Avery's hands.

But Avery could tell that Nadia was loving it.

"Maybe just a little further," Avery went on, pulling the fabric down even further to expose more of Nadia's ass. Instead of pretending to fight it, Nadia simply wiggled her rear and got comfortable in the sheets.

It wasn't long before Avery was completely pulling Nadia's underwear off of her rear, down her legs, and removing them from her feet. She tossed them over her shoulder and once more climbed up the length of Nadia's legs until she closed in again on her ass. Avery pressed her hands firmly onto Nadia's cheeks. She squeezed and massaged them, she pulled them apart, she rubbed them up and down.

"That's nice," cooed Nadia.

"You should see it from my angle," Avery said. Nadia laughed.

"It's pretty good, isn't it?"

"Really good," agreed Avery. "You've got a very hot ass." Leaning down slowly, Avery planted a soft kiss on one of Nadia's cheeks.

"You know what I like," Nadia said in a low, sultry tone. The feeling in the room had changed from teasing fun to seduction. Avery grinned and nodded slowly.

Avery licked her thumb and then she placed her hand

on Nadia's rump. She pushed her thumb between Nadia's cheeks and settled it onto her asshole, beginning to then massage it in pressured, steady circles.

"Oh God," said Nadia. She pressed her face into the pillows once again and relaxed. The feeling of Avery's thumb against the sensitivity of her ass made her head swim with arousal. She could feel the heat growing within her middle.

"I love making you happy," mused Avery, watching herself as she fondled Nadia from behind. She brought her free hand to her own breast and touched herself through the tensile fabric of her top.

The women just clicked in bed. There was no shame or shyness at this point. They drove each other wild and it showed. While some people never broke down the barriers of their fantasies, Nadia and Avery were both eager to please. As Avery continued pressing her thumb firmly against her lover, massaging it round and round, she began to get intoxicated off of Nadia's passionate groans and her eager writhing.

Feeling herself begin to sweat, Avery halted in her stroking, raised her hands up, and removed her camisole. Her pert breasts tumbled out, she tossed her top off the bed, yet remained straddled on Nadia now in just her lacy shorts. Nadia looked behind herself and when she saw Avery topless she grinned. Beginning to maneuver out from under Avery, Nadia flipped herself over so that her full front was now exposed to her lover.

"This looks so tasty," intoned Avery, her fingers running

through Nadia's fur. Nadia moved a leg and widened her stance, exposing herself to Avery and inviting her in.

"I'm already pretty wet," said Nadia. She smiled seductively at Avery as Avery raised her brow.

"I can see that," said Avery. She reached her hand down and slowly dragged a single finger upward in Nadia's slit, gliding easily through the wet flesh. Nadia shuddered in pleasure.

"Oh God," said Nadia. "I just want you to fuck me so bad." Nadia had a look of intense longing on her face, like she'd never been more eager for sex in her life. This look made Avery feel her own heart begin to race with excitement.

"You just reminded me," said Avery, changing gears. Nadia watched with interest as Avery leapt up from the bed and ran out of the room, wearing nothing but her shorts.

To Nadia, it felt like forever before Avery returned. But when Avery came back into the room, Nadia's eyes widened as she looked at what Avery had brought with her.

Avery grinned and held up what looked like a black leather harness belt. Jutting out from the front of it was a stiff purple totem with a slight curve to it. Nadia immediately knew what this was and she sat up quickly in bed, her expression full of suspense and wonderment.

"Is that what I think that is?" Nadia asked.

"It is," said Avery, stepping closer to the bed, and looking down at the toy she carried in her hand. "I'm glad you didn't go through my shipping boxes and ruin the surprise."

"You had *that* sent from New York?" said Nadia in disbelief.

"Among other things," said Avery. "Do you want to try it?"

Nadia nodded eagerly.

Avery tossed the strap to the bed as she quickly pushed down her shorts, giving Nadia a moment to inspect it. It had a belt with two straps to go around Avery's legs, and the purple dildo affixed to it had two sides. One was long and upright, while the other was almost like a bulb. Nadia felt slightly confused by it.

"What is that part?" Nadia asked, pointing at it. "The bulb?"

"That goes inside me," Avery said and grinned wildly. "And the whole piece vibrates when you turn it on."

"That is definitely exciting," said Nadia, still surveying the toy. She was absentmindedly playing with her own tit as she watched Avery now pick up the strap and get herself into it.

Avery stepped into it and pulled the harness up her legs. As she brought it upward, she placed one foot on the bed and took hold of the dildo. Nadia watched, eyes big, as Avery guided the bulb side against herself, and with a slight bit of pressure it parted her lips and disappeared inside of her.

"Mmm," hummed Avery, gyrating her hips. She then wrapped the belt around her waist and fastened it, making sure to pull it tightly so that it was snug and secure.

"How does that feel?" Nadia said softly.

"Good," said Avery. "It'll feel even better once I turn this thing on."

"My God," said Nadia. "I can't even believe this. I'm so turned on right now watching you put that thing on." Reaching down, Nadia felt herself between the legs. She had become quite slippery.

"Perfect," Avery replied, grinning wide and climbing up onto the bed. "Are you ready to have one of your fantasies fulfilled?"

Again, another eager and excited nod from Nadia. She spread herself out and watched Avery's face intently. Avery mounted Nadia now, her eyes focused on the dildo between her legs, and she navigated herself closer to her lover. Nadia's heart was racing, feeling like it could just leap out of her chest. One of her hands gripped tightly to the sheets in anticipation.

Reaching underneath the device, Avery flipped a switch and the dildo began to buzz. She squirmed and made a small intonation of pleasure. Then she looked up at Nadia and smiled.

"It's really vibrating," said Avery.

With her hand around the base of the dildo, Avery pressed it against Nadia's pussy. Both women watched the action with aroused hunger. As the purple piece split Nadia's lips and began its move inside of her, she could immediately feel the vibrations. Once it slipped half-way inside, all Nadia could do was drop her head to the pillows and accept it. As soon as Avery began to pump against her, Nadia was transported to another world.

Nadia laid there in the bed, head to the side, legs akimbo, as Avery perched atop her. Avery had her hands on Nadia's shoulders, and she thrust into her, hard and steady and methodically. Nadia could feel her breathing quicken, and she held onto herself with a single hand against her upper chest. Her body rocked back and forth as Avery fucked her. The thick, firm yet malleable toy buzzed inside of her. It felt incredible. Nadia's stomach clenched.

Both women were groaning and grunting and squirming, the pleasure they felt was reciprocal and similar. The silicone bulb inside of Avery buzzed along with the dildo, and she could feel her own desire and arousal growing at an identical pace to Nadia. Nadia reached a hand up and held tightly to Avery's arm, which gave Avery a bit more steadiness to push harder.

The immense longing of love flooded Nadia's mind. She was high on passion, drunk on lust. The tingle in her belly grew with each thrust of Avery's hips. Nadia was close, she could feel it. Her toes curled and her butt wiggled into her bed, a damp spot just under her on the sheet. Opening her eyes, Nadia looked upward and she locked eyes with Avery. Neither woman said anything. They just moaned along with their breath, and they looked deeply into each other's eyes. They were focused and determined.

When Nadia began to come, her movements were violent and thrashing. It was the best orgasm of her life and she felt like she was falling. Reaching out with both hands, she dug her fingers into the sheets in search of solid ground. Her hips jolted back and forth, and even though during these motions the dildo slipped out of her, the intensity of orgasm wouldn't cease.

"Oh fuck," said Nadia, her face sweaty and concerned, her body almost convulsing. "Oh fuck."

Nadia opened her eyes slowly, eager to see Avery, and she saw her lover perched in front of her, on her knees. Avery's eyes were closed, and her hand was pressing down on the dildo, which caused the bulb in her pussy to press firmly against her on the inside. Her body was sporadically jolting as well, and Nadia wanted nothing more than for the love of her life to come as she had.

She reached out and she gripped to the purple toy. Nadia pulled it downwards, just as Avery was doing. Avery opened her eyes, a lust-drunk expression on her face, and she knew immediately what Nadia was doing. Bringing both hands up, Avery began to play with her own nipples as she succumbed to the fervent vibrations inside of her.

"Come for me," whispered Nadia.

And Avery did. Her hips bounced side to side as orgasmic electricity coursed through her. She felt sweat under her arms, and under her knees, and she was drenched between her legs from her own arousal. The bulb continued vibrating methodically through the climax, and soon it was too much for Avery to bear. She began laughing maniacally, ripping at the buckle of the belt, trying to get it off.

"It's too much," she said. "It's too much." Nadia just watched with intense interest.

Avery was able to get the buckle unlatched, and as she pushed the harness down off of her hips, the purple bulb easily popped out of her glistening slit. She took a deep breath and raised a hand to her chest to steady herself. The skin above her breasts was reddened. After a moment, Avery collapsed down into the bed, next to Nadia, and she continued breathing heavily.

"It's still buzzing," teased Nadia, now lightly kissing Avery all over her face.

"Oh," Avery said in momentary confusion. Once she realized what Nadia had said, she reached between her legs and searched for the switch on the dildo. The buzzing noise ceased.

The women laid together, the only sound was there labored and syncopated breathing. They lazily intertwined with each other, haphazardly holding on as their hearts slowed and they came back down from the clouds.

"That was incredible," Nadia said after a moment.

"You're incredible," said Avery. Her eyes were closed, her forehead slightly wrinkled. Nadia could tell that Avery was still feeling something, still experiencing the aftershocks.

"I want to fuck you with that thing," said Nadia, her hand on Avery's arm, petting her tenderly.

"Just give me a minute," said Avery. She opened her eyes and offered an exasperated smile. "I love you."

"I love you," said Nadia.

They nuzzled into one another, their bodies finally relaxing. The smell of love and sex was in the air. And for these two lovers, it was only the beginning of their journey together. There was so much more in front of them.

Nadia couldn't stop smiling. And neither could Avery.

NADIA WALKED through the door of the yoga studio, though she was dressed in her street clothes. She felt at ease, happy, as she had had a leisurely morning after making breakfast for Avery and seeing her off to work. There was a class going on in the studio's backroom, which was partitioned off from the reception area. Sitting behind the desk was a woman who looked to be a very young fifty, and Nadia knew her as the owner of the studio.

"Good morning," she said, her long hair, streaked with gray, pulled back in a loose bun. "Nadia, right?"

"Yes," said Nadia with a smile, stepping up to the desk. "Yvonne?"

"That's me," Yvonne replied with a small laugh. "How can I help you today?"

"Well, I've been thinking it over," Nadia said. "And I'd like to sign up for teacher training. There's an upcoming session, isn't there?"

"Yes there is," said Yvonne, her smile easy and blithe. "That's wonderful, Nadia. We will be so happy to have you join us."

"How many people are in the training program?" Nadia asked, setting her small bag up on the counter.

"You will make it nine," said Yvonne.

"Is a woman named Ellen enrolled, do you know?"

"Ellen?" repeated Yvonne. "The blonde woman? Yes, she certainly is."

"Oh, that's great," said Nadia. She felt excited by this

prospect. This was a whole new chapter for her and it really made her feel alive.

"Now, it's a three month program," said Yvonne, pulling out a clipboard with some paperwork attached to it. She slid the clipboard across the desk to Nadia, who in turn picked it up and began to look it over. "It's intensive, and we do meet five days a week during the day. Does that work with your schedule?"

"It does," said Nadia, picking up a pen and beginning to fill out the form.

"What is your yoga background?" Yvonne asked. "Have you been practicing long?"

"In college I did it often," Nadia said. "And it's been off an on over the years, more so in my late twenties than recently. But since losing my job, I've been at it a lot more."

"Oh, I'm sorry to hear about your job loss," Yvonne said empathetically.

"It's fine," Nadia reassured her, looking up from the paperwork and smiling. "It's actually been a blessing."

"Sometimes the universe gives us exactly what we need, exactly when we need it," Yvonne said happily. Nadia, still smiling, nodded in agreement.

"It felt strange at first," said Nadia. "But I'm really happy that things have turned out as they have."

"We're all on our own unique journey," said Yvonne. "Isn't that wonderful to know?"

"It really is," said Nadia in earnest. She smiled for a moment, considering Yvonne's words, and then she returned to filling out the form.

"I wouldn't have started this studio if I hadn't been laid off from my job all those years ago," said Yvonne. "I could very well still be an accountant right now!" She laughed at this notion, the expression on her face conveying how glad she was about where she ended up.

"No job is really all that safe, is it?" mused Nadia. "You think you're doing okay and then *wham!*"

"Yes, I find that it's far better to do what you love for less money than to do something that's falsely secure that you have no control over," Yvonne said. "You only get one shot at this life, better make it count!"

"Right," said Nadia. She looked over the paperwork, double-checking that everything she had written was correct, and then she handed it back to Yvonne.

"Thank you," said Yvonne, smiling as she looked over the sheet. "Thank you, Nadia Marek. Namaste."

"You're welcome," replied Nadia, smiling along with Yvonne.

"Now the fee is five thousand dollars," Yvonne said. "Which includes everything for the entire three months. You'll also have unlimited access to all classes at the studio, so even after you've completed your training for the day, you could still come back and drop in on another class."

"That's great," said Nadia, pulling her checkbook out of her purse. She quickly wrote the check, ripped it from the book, and handed it over to Yvonne.

"Thank you very much," said Yvonne. She paper-clipped the check to Nadia's paperwork.

"So what now?" Nadia asked. "I'm excited to begin."

"We'll be starting two Mondays from now," said Yvonne. "I'll be sending out an email shortly with all the scheduling."

"That's terrific," said Nadia. "Well, okay then. I guess I'll see you in two Mondays."

"Definitely," said Yvonne. "Thank you once again, Nadia," she said, putting her palms together and bowing her head. "I look forward to our time together."

"I do, too," said Nadia, smiling big and feeling real joy in making this decision. "I really do."

When Nadia stepped back outside into the late summer sun, she was smiling wide as she put her sunglasses over her eyes and began walking down the street and back toward her building. She eagerly pulled her phone from her bag, quickly moved through her contacts, and pushed the call button. The phone rang as she held it against her ear, still walking, still smiling.

The phone made a clicking sound and then Avery answered.

"My dearest," Avery said joyfully. "Did you do it?"

"I did it," Nadia affirmed. "It feels so great to make that decision. I was all over the place for too long, and it was beginning to drive me nuts. But this feels right. I'm really excited for this yoga training."

"I'm happy for you," said Avery. "Truly, I am. Change like this can be scary, but you must do what you feel is right for you."

"I could not have done this without you," Nadia said. "Really, I couldn't."

"Oh, is that because I came into your job and made you redundant?" joked Avery. Nadia laughed.

"God, isn't that crazy?" she replied. "I really can't believe how this all started and how we got to this point. It wasn't even all that long ago, but I feel like a completely different person."

"Yes, but it all worked out very well in the end," Avery continued. "It was a bumpy ride — for both of us, really — but I think this is about the best ending we could ask for."

"I wish you had been able to get what you wanted, though," said Nadia.

"Forget about that," Avery countered quickly. "I'm perfectly content with this. It's actually quite a relief to be free from that incessant corporate climb. I am an extremely fortunate woman. I have my health, I'm very well-off financially, and... I have love in my life." Nadia smiled so large that it almost made her face ache.

"I love you so much, Avery," said Nadia. "Thank you for coming into my life."

"I love *you*," Avery said. "This has been a dream come true for me, really it has."

"I'll see you at home later tonight," Nadia said.

"Yes, indeed," said Avery. "Congratulations on your next step, my love."

"Thank you," said Nadia. "See you later, babe."

"See you tonight," Avery said.

Nadia hung up the phone, and she dropped it back into her purse. Stopping where she was on the sidewalk, she placed a hand over her heart, and she looked up in the sky. She was grinning.

She felt like the luckiest woman alive.

———————

THREE MONTHS LATER...

NADIA WALKED up to her condo door wearing a thin purple puffy jacket, tight black leggings, sneakers, and she had her rolled yoga mat hung over her shoulder. Her hair was back in a ponytail and she had an elastic strip headband across her forehead. She looked as though she had just exerted herself to exhaustion, her cheeks pink, her face plain and make-up free. There was a satisfied smile on her lips, she looked happy and spent. Pushing her key into the lock, Nadia opened the door and stepped inside.

As she entered the condo and dropped her yoga mat to the floor near the entrance, she could hear that Avery was on the phone at the couch. She was talking on speakerphone, her laptop and phone sitting on the coffee table, while Avery sat at the edge of the couch and spoke.

"I think we could make a bid on the South Wacker building if we partner with Stone Properties," said Avery. She smiled as she saw Nadia come in and she waved. Nadia happily waved back.

"Yes, I agree," said the voice coming through the phone. It was Charles, Avery's father. "Stone has always been an agreeable partner for joint ventures, and this deal seems right up their alley."

Nadia had removed her coat and slipped off her shoes, and she left the living area and entered the bathroom. She dropped her hands to the hem of her tank top and she pulled it off over her head, tossing it into a hamper. Standing there in just a sports bra and her yoga pants, she smiled at herself in the mirror. She felt truly as though she was looking a lot healthier since she'd begun yoga teacher training. Giving up much of her alcohol consumption was a good move, and her face looked much less puffy because of it. Her eyes were brighter, her smile easier and more earnest. She felt beautiful, and she felt happy.

Exiting the bathroom, she returned to the main area with the intent to go to the kitchen for a glass of water. But the conversation she heard Avery and her father having stopped her in her path, and made her instead change direction and walk closer into the living room.

"I have been working closely with Max," said Charles through the speakerphone. "As I anticipate my retirement in another handful of years. However, I do believe he still has much to learn about being in command. He struggles, at times, with confidence when leading a meeting."

"Yes," agreed Avery. "I understand what you're saying."

Nadia crossed her arms, listened, and hovered off to the side. Avery looked to her for a moment to acknowledge her, but then she looked back at her laptop, simply staring forward as she spoke with her father.

"I've been thinking more about this situation," Charles

continued. "And I am willing to speak with you further about the possibility of making you CEO of M. M. Wool Properties. Provided it is something that you still count among your professional interests."

"Well, I..." Avery stumbled, taken aback by her father's words. "Yes. I mean, that is certainly an idea I would entertain."

"This would be some time down the road, mind you," said Charles. "I am not ready to retire yet. But I am looking toward the future, and despite the fact that Max is a very capable contract lawyer and keen investor, his leadership abilities leave something to be desired. And leadership abilities are something you have, Avery, in spades."

"Thank you for saying so," Avery replied. She looked to Nadia with wide, surprised eyes and she shrugged. Nadia smiled and nodded enthusiastically. "I appreciate your kind words."

"Of course," said Charles. "So please, I urge you to consider it and we can speak more about the possibility at a later date. For now, let's continue exploring our options with purchasing the building on South Wacker."

"Yes, let's," said Avery. "I'll reach out to Daria at Stone Properties first thing tomorrow morning and speak to her about a joint partnership on this deal."

"Terrific," said Charles. "Thank you very much, Avery."

"You're welcome," she said.

"Goodbye, Avery."

"Goodbye, Dad."

Avery reached to the table and pressed her phone

screen. She then quickly looked to Nadia, offering another expression of surprise, and she stood up.

"Did you hear that?" Avery asked.

"I did," Nadia replied, smiling as she felt Avery's excitement.

"I didn't just imagine that, did I?" said Avery. "He's talking about handing the company over to me now?"

"That's what I heard," said Nadia.

"Well, isn't that something?" Avery mused. She smiled and she shook her head as it sunk in.

"What would it mean?" asked Nadia. "Would you need to be back in New York?"

"I think it would," said Avery. "But, like you heard my father say, this would still be years down the road. I know you love Chicago and you aren't interested in leaving."

"You know," said Nadia. "This yoga training has really changed my perspective on some things. I don't know what happened, but I definitely feel more adventurous lately. I don't think it really matters where you are at all. You can be happy anywhere you happen to be, as long as you make the choice to be happy."

"So if I had to return to New York eventually," said Avery. "You would consider accompanying me?"

"Most definitely," Nadia said, she was grinning and she looked completely content.

"Nadia, you are the best," said Avery. She stepped closer to Nadia, wrapped her arms around her tightly, and the two of them deeply and lovingly kissed. It was obvious that they had something special between them, a growing knowledge of who the other one was, a mutual respect, and a real love that doesn't just happen every day. They were proof that love could prevail in difficult, and sometimes strange, circumstances.

When their kiss came to its natural conclusion, Nadia smiled happily, looking into Avery's eyes.

"This has all been the best and most surprising experience of my life," admitted Nadia. "Last spring, I was on such a completely different track than I am now as we head into winter. It just… it's so unexpected and so exciting. I'm about to finish yoga teacher training, I've never felt more healthy, I've never felt more happy, and I've never felt more like I'm on the right track."

"This has all been quite a surprise for me as well," said Avery. "It's funny how quickly things can change, how different your life can get from where you were previously, and how natural it can all feel. I am grateful for our journey together. This has meant the world to me."

The women kissed once again, and then they stood there in the living room embracing one another in a comfortable silence. They were both happy, and they were both in love. And the best part, the greatest feeling of all, was that it felt like their wonderful love affair had only just begun.

Thank you for reading!

If you enjoyed this novel,
please leave a review!

Reviews are *super* important!
Your review can help Nico
reach more readers!

Even if you're not the wordy type,
leaving a review saying
"I really enjoyed this book!"
is still incredibly helpful.

Pretty please?

If you want to be notified
of all new releases from Nico,
sign up for her mailing list today
and get 3 FREE STORIES!

Point your web browser
to the following address
and sign up right now!

https://readni.co

Keep reading to see more books from
Nicolette Dane!

A WAY WITH WORDS

Evelyn Driscoll, famed novelist and professor at a small midwestern arts college, has been feeling lost. It's been over seven years since her hit book came out, her editor is clamoring for a new manuscript, and life in northern Ohio just doesn't compare to the literary world she once inhabited. Her love life feels like even more of a mess. Evie is really beginning to feel trapped.

When one of her graduate writing students, the beautiful and talented Meadow Sims, makes her adoration known, Evie feels the passion she once had for life and love all start coming back. Meadow is smart, sweet, and she has almost completed a novel of her own. But Evie and

Meadow must thread the needle carefully, keeping their romance hidden from a jealous rival student and the university administration.

Can this love affair succeed despite the professional consequences? Will love win out over jealousy and prohibition? Blossoming love can be a catalyst for change, and accepting everything that change entails isn't always the easiest proposition. But it could be exactly what Evie needs.

www.nicolettedane.com

AN ACT OF LOVE

When Jessica Coleridge arrives in Los Angeles to open her new yoga studio, the only person she knows in town is her old friend Liberty Logan. To Jessica's surprise, Liberty has become a famous television actress on a hit comedy show. As the friends rekindle what they once had, romance begins to flourish and this reunion between Jessica and Liberty quickly evolves into much more than friendship.

But fame and money begin to play tricks on Liberty, as she's still naive to her growing celebrity. And with Jessica reentering her life out of the blue, Liberty has a difficult time determining what's real and what's just an act. When money and business get involved with love and romance, even old friends can let their emotions get the better of them.

Will this second chance at love for Jessica and Liberty persevere through the trappings of Hollywood, fame, and money? Can these two women see past the noise all around them and accept their feelings for one another? Celebrity can be tricky and confusing, but love has the power to overcome it all... if only we can listen to our hearts.

www.nicolettedane.com

FIELD DAY

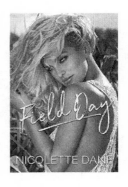

After getting into some trouble in the big city, Jane Cairns is sent to live with her aunt and uncle on the family farm. She's lost in life, worried, stranded, living in a state of arrested development as she ambles through her young adulthood. A normal twenty six year old woman should be able to flourish on her own, but Jane can't seem to make things work.

Farm life begins to show Jane a different side when she meets Sally Harris. Sally is a proud farm girl, in love with her country life, and happy to work at her family's cherry orchard. Things can be a bit stifling in the country, however, when it comes to love. And coming out from behind that barrier isn't something Sally knows how to do.

Each battling their own issues of identity and place, Jane and Sally struggle together to find out what it means to be free and happy. Will they be able to survive Jane's dirty past, secret love, family and friendship, and even death? Love is a tender and delicate thing, and it's something we all deserve. But the path to get there isn't always as straight as we might think.

www.nicolettedane.com

FLOATS HER BOAT

After her mother's passing, Brooke Nilsson makes the trek up to her family's Minnesota vacation home to clean up the clutter and prepare the cabin for sale. Brooke never considered herself to be very outdoorsy, much preferring her big city life to lounging on the lake, and she's not looking forward to spending her summer in the middle of nowhere.

But when she meets her neighbor, famous singer Hailey Reed, Brooke's feelings begin to change about her old family getaway. Hailey, the beautiful and sultry redhead songbird, shows Brooke just how much fun lakeside living can be. And as the summer fun takes a romantic turn, Brooke can't help but question the way she's felt about the cabin for so long.

With a generous offer on the table, will Brooke be able to pull the trigger and sell her family's cabin? Or will her newfound love of the home, and her growing feelings for Hailey, prevent her from going through with the sale? Sometimes the stories we tell about ourselves are nothing more than stories, and our feelings about who we are can change when we least expect it.

www.nicolettedane.com

LOVE & WANDERLUST

Julia Marks isn't one to stick around very long. She's blissfully living the vanlife, crossing the country as she pleases, working odd jobs to fund her lifestyle, treading lightly, and leaving no trace behind her. But despite the immense freedom she has as a traveling nomad, she can't help but feel that something's missing... perhaps *someone*.

A quick trip through Madison turns far more interesting for Julia when she meets Robin Hyland. Robin is searching for answers, and a chance encounter between the two women opens up a brand new adventure that neither expected. While Julia didn't anticipate having a passenger in her van, it's hard to say no to a pretty redhead who's looking to find herself.

Will Julia and Robin be able to navigate the potentially treacherous road ahead of them and come out unscathed? Can love win out over the demons that both women must face? Life on the road has its challenges, especially when you're living the bohemian life in your van. Facing those obstacles with a partner, however, might reveal a route never before considered.

www.nicolettedane.com

TINY HOUSE BIG LOVE

After being laid off from her job at a law firm, Maxine Thune finds herself questioning her direction and looking for a change. She has lived out the typical life script. Max has the big house and the nice car, all the various trappings of material success, and she also has the debt to prove it. With this job loss, however, she's uncertain how she'll continue to afford it all.

But when Cadence Walsh comes into her life, the script is flipped for Max. Cady is a beautiful and free-spirited yoga teacher, she's a hippie, and she lives in a tiny house out in the woods. With no debts, few worries, and a more serene life, Cady reminds Max of her own bohemian past and she shows Max what their future could hold together.

Can Max ditch her life of over-consumption, learn to live small, and find tranquility in a tiny house? Will going tiny be the change Max needs to discover her authentic self? Just because a home is small, that doesn't mean the love within its walls can't be big. And sometimes removing what's unnecessary from our lives is the key to finding that which we truly need to grow.

www.nicolettedane.com

RESTLESS ON A ROAD TRIP

Having just finalized the divorce from her husband, Dana Darling feels uncertain and lost in life. As a woman in her mid-30s, where does she go from here? How does she move on? Dana knows the divorce was the right thing to do and these feelings inside can no longer be ignored. She's certain real love is out there for her... but how can she find it?

When her good friend Maggie invites her on a road trip out west, Dana's eyes begin to open. Maggie is a firecracker, a sweet, pretty, and sensual woman who Dana has always admired. And while Maggie has always been open about her own love of women, Dana has never been able to come out to her friend and admit her true feelings. Dana is about to find out, however, that when you're on the open road with a fun and flirty woman like Maggie, things have a way of coming out like they never have before.

Will the freedom Dana feels on this road trip vacation allow her to finally open up and be free herself? Can this liberation from the responsibilities of life set Dana on the path she was meant to travel all along? Or will the coming out Dana has always deserved continue to be under construction? Some road blocks in life are difficult to navigate. But for Dana the call of the open road is too deafening to dismiss.

www.nicolettedane.com

GIVE ME SOME SUGAR

With the dream of owning her own bakery finally coming together, Angie West finds herself struggling with life as a business owner. She's overworked and underpaid, trying to figure out how she can take the bakery to the next level, balance all her money problems, and do so without sacrificing her mostly non-existent love life. Does an entrepreneur ever get a break?

Luckily, one of her customers is ready and eager to help. Ellen Liu runs her own business consultancy, the exact thing Angie and her bakery need. In addition to being bright, enthusiastic, and clever, Ellen is also a stunningly beautiful woman. And Angie, in a moment of weakness, finds herself kneading Ellen into a small fib to impress her biggest investor. Angie is totally smitten with her new partner, and it's coming out in the most half-baked way.

Can Angie get past her issues with family, money, and work, and allow love to prevail with Ellen? Will their relationship of convenience develop into much more than either woman thought possible? Or will this confection connection end up bittersweet? Angie's sure that Ellen's the one for her... now if only she can rise to the occasion.

www.nicolettedane.com

FULL BODIED IN THE VINEYARD

After yet another breakup and on the cusp of her 40th birthday, Shannon Laughlin is feeling lost. Life hasn't gone quite how she expected and she's ready for something new, a new outlook, a new adventure. A new love. One night, as she tries to figure out what's next, a chance post on social media by an old friend offers to give her that change she's been seeking.

That old friend is Alina. Alina is a seasonal worker at Wild Love Winery up on Leelanau Peninsula in Michigan's wine appellation. A free-spirited woman, Alina has orchestrated a life for herself that revolves around following her bliss. It's something Shan has always admired in her friend.

That, and Alina's undeniable sensuality. Shan can't help but remember the one night in college that the two women shared a bed. And the possibility Alina is offering is just too good to pass up.

Will Shan figure out how to get both her work life and her love life back on track as she stumbles into her 40s? Can the magic of Michigan's wine country and the surrounding beauty convince Shan that there's more to this world than she's been able to see? Or will this second chance at making it work with Alina prove to be out of her reach? Sometimes life is only just beginning at 40, as Shan is about to find out. And there's so much more of it to live.

www.nicolettedane.com

AN EXCERPT: A WAY WITH WORDS

"Take a syllabus from the pile and pass the rest," said Evelyn Driscoll, standing at the front of the classroom. Evelyn, or Evie as most people called her, was a tall, slim, and elegant woman nearing forty. Dressed in a black turtleneck, a wool skirt, black tights, and knee-high boots, she not only looked very put together but also quite hip. She pursed her lips as she watched the students, numbering about fifteen, take their syllabus, pass the pile, and then look down into the pages.

After a moment, Evie handed out another sheet.

"On this page coming around," began Evie. "You'll see a schedule of workshop critiques. Sign your name to it and we'll have the order. Each of you will get three critiques this semester."

One student raised his hand, a timid looking guy with wire glasses and a thin beard.

"Yes?" said Evie in his direction.

"If the sign up sheet goes around the room," said the young man, indicating with his finger to the students that sat in a square around tables fitted together. "Doesn't that mean the last person to sign up really has no choice?"

"That's right," Evie said with a spark in her eye. "That's just how it goes sometimes."

The young man slowly nodded and then looked down into his syllabus.

"We'll also be reading a handful of novels this semester," Evie said. "The syllabus will tell you when you should have them read by. Generally speaking, class will go like this: about a half-hour discussing the novel, and then a half-hour for each of the three students receiving critiques on their work. That should fill our two hours each week."

Evie crossed her arms underneath her breasts and looked around the room, waiting to see if any more questions would arise. These students should know the ropes by now, as this was the second semester of their first year in grad school. They had already done a writing workshop with other professors prior to Evie's class, though teaching styles could vary wildly between instructors. However, Evie ran her class in a pretty standard manner and besides, many of these students had probably taken writing workshops when they were in college.

Another hand slowly raised. It belonged to a beautiful young woman with dark hair and dark eyes, contrasted with pale skin and lips coated with a dark pink lipstick. Evie felt her heart flutter when she looked on at the woman, and the attraction she felt was immediate. But Evie was professional, or at least trying to be lately, and never got involved with students. Besides, there had been a shakeup in the English department not too long ago with a professor and student having a relationship, and it did not end well. Evie was careful with her career. She had to be.

"Yes?" Evie said. The pretty young woman looked up to Evie and smiled big.

"Hi," she said. "Do you know if any of the authors on your reading list will be at Book Bash at the end of the semester?"

Book Bash was a writing festival that the university hosted, bringing in authors and publishers from all over the country. It was a week-long event, filled with talks and work-shops and parties. It was a way for the writing students, and the local community as a whole, to mingle with working writers and even shop their own work around with editors and agents to try to get published.

"I think the schedule is still being finalized," said Evie to the woman, raising an eyebrow in her direction. "But yes, I've included a few authors I know will be in attendance to give you all a leg up if you happen to speak with them."

"Thank you," said the young woman, giving Evie another big smile. There was something magnetic about her, something undeniably fun exuding from her.

Evie noticed that the young woman held a red pen in her fingers. And when the critique sign-up sheet came to her, she signed up with that red pen. Evie was suddenly desperate to know her name, and she kept an eye on the sheet as it continued around the room.

"Why don't we go around in a circle, introduce ourselves, and talk a little bit about what we write and our influences," said Evie, still watching the sign up sheet move. "I'll go first. I'm Evie Driscoll, I've been a professor here at Westin for almost six years. Some of you may know me from my novel, *The Hyacinth Hotel*—"

When Evie mentioned her book, a few of the students started to clap. The rest joined in after a moment. It wasn't a rousing applause or anything like that, just a small congratulations. The novel had actually been a big deal, had won some awards, and it put Evie on the map. But it had been some time since *The Hyacinth Hotel* had come out. Evie gave a half-smile.

"Thank you," she said. "That's very sweet of you all. I'm surprised you all remember it." The students laughed. "Anyhow, that's me. And I'll be your instructor this semester. Next…" Evie said, motioning to the young man sitting to her right.

As the student began speaking, the sign up sheet reached Evie and she looked down into it, searching quickly for the name written in red ink. Meadow Sims was her name, and as soon as Evie read it she lifted her eyes and gazed across the room at Meadow once again. Meadow's eyes were pointed to the speaking student, but after a moment they looked to the front of the classroom and met directly with Evie's. Evie quickly looked away, averting her attention to the speaking student and hoping that Meadow hadn't really caught her staring.

However, Evie couldn't help but feel impatient for the introductions to move around the table and get to Meadow. She chastised herself the whole time. *You're crazy, Evie*, she thought to herself. *Don't do this to yourself.*

"I'm Meadow Sims," Meadow said once it was her turn, smiling and raising her hand slightly, eyes looking around the room. "I'm a fan of Jennifer Egan, Jhumpa Lahiri, and well, um… Evelyn Driscoll," she said, sheepishly shrugging and indicating toward Evie. "I'm working on a novel, so I'll be sharing parts of that with you all. And, uh, I really like doughnuts." Meadow grinned and the class laughed.

Evie smiled across the room at Meadow, and Meadow caught her looking once again.

"Thank you, Meadow," Evie said.

It wasn't much longer until class ended, as they had nothing more to talk about until the writing critiques began. Once Evie dismissed the students, everybody began standing up, collecting their things, and slipping into their coats.

"Check your email tonight," said Evie over the commotion of the students preparing to leave. "I'll send out a list of everybody's email, as well as this schedule. Those of you going first next week, make sure to get your work to us all by Friday," she said. "Got it? No later than Friday at noon."

Evie smiled and watched as the students all ushered themselves out of the classroom. Some looked on to her with reverence as they passed, while some other avoided eye contact all together. She had gotten used to it. Evie was one of the big names teaching at Westin, and it wasn't unheard of for students to attend Westin for their Master of Fine Arts graduate degree specifically to work with her. However, as the time between the present and the publication of *The Hyacinth Hotel* grew larger, the pressure for a successful follow-up novel grew at a similar rate, and the number of students coming to Westin to study with Evie dwindled.

As Evie dwelled on all these thoughts, she was shaken from her reverie by Meadow appearing directly in front of her. The class had completely emptied but for the two of them. Evie was surprised, eyes wide, as she looked at Meadow. And Meadow looked back at Evie with hope and joy in her face.

"Hi," said Meadow finally. "I don't know if you remember my name," she started. "But I'm Meadow Sims." Meadow extended her hand.

Evie looked down to Meadow's hand, paused for a moment, and then shook.

"It's very nice to meet you, Meadow," said Evie. "I noticed you signed the list with a red pen."

"Yeah," Meadow said with a curt laugh. "I just like using a red pen for whatever reason."

"If you mark up the other students' writing with red ink," Evie said. "The criticism might not feel as gentle as blue or black ink. You get what I'm saying?"

"I understand," Meadow said and nodded. "But I only

buy red pens, so..." Her expression grew impish and excited.

Evie grinned and chuckled softly.

"So be it," acquiesced Evie.

"I just wanted to tell you how wonderful it is to finally meet you," Meadow said. "I hope I don't seem like a nutty super-fan or anything, but *The Hyacinth Hotel* is what made me really want to be a writer. I read it in a contemporary literature class my first year in college," she said. "The year it came out."

"That was seven years ago," Evie mused.

"Right," said Meadow. "Seven years ago."

"It's been some time, huh?" said Evie.

"Yes," agreed Meadow. "I can't wait for your next novel. Is it going to be out soon, or...?"

"I'm still working on it," said Evie. "I don't really have a set date yet."

"Okay," said Meadow through an earnest smile. She tucked some of her dark hair behind her ear. "Well, I'll buy it the moment it comes out. I can't wait."

"Thank you, Meadow," Evie said. She offered the student a weak smile and a gentle nod.

"I know this is a bit forward," Meadow said, averting her eyes for a moment. But any kind of embarrassment that reared itself inside of her was quickly vanquished, and Meadow looked back to Evie with a greater sense of resolve. "Next year, when we have to get together with a thesis group and pick an advisor, I was wondering if you would be my advisor."

"Well, that's an entire year away, Meadow," said Evie. "And I haven't even read any of your work yet. We might not even mesh well, you know? We might butt heads in class."

"Oh," said Meadow, her attitude dampening for a moment. "Yeah, I suppose that's true."

"And besides," Evie said. "We really don't even get into that until the end of first semester next year. Right now, I'm working with my current crop of thesis students."

"I understand," said Meadow, her positivity returning. "I'm just trying to get a jump on it all."

"I appreciate that," said Evie, mirroring the smile on Meadow's face.

"I'm actually almost done with my novel," admitted Meadow. "I started it the summer before I came to school here."

"Oh?" said Evie. "Did you workshop it last semester, too?"

"I did," Meadow said. "Workshop has been really helpful."

"Well, I look forward to reading it," said Evie. Evie picked up her coat, a thick black quilted down jacket that went down to her ankles, and slipped into it. "But for now, I should probably get moving."

"Oh, right," said Meadow. "Me too. Thank you, Professor Driscoll," she said with a smile. "I'm so excited for your class." Meadow's eyes sparkled as she admired her professor.

"Evie," Evie replied. "You can call me Evie if you like."

"Evie," said Meadow, grinning and nodding. "That's great."

"Have a wonderful afternoon, Meadow," said Evie. She picked up her bag and slung it over her shoulder.

"You too," said Meadow, still smiling. After another moment, Meadow turned from Evie and exited the classroom. Evie sighed and relaxed, looking up toward the ceiling. It was so hard to deny the pretty, doting students that came through her classes. And Meadow might have been one of the worst of them. The girl was gorgeous and bright. Evie could only hope that Meadow was a terrible writer, because if she was good... well, it might be hard to hold herself back.

It was bright white and snowy outside, but it was warm and cozy as Evie walked into Half Mast, a bar and restaurant just off the main drag across from the university. Half Mast was nautical themed, very wooden and quaint inside, yet a little more upscale from the other bars in town. That, and the slightly raised prices, kept most of the students out. It was a tavern frequented by the professors and other townies. Evie smiled, feeling almost immediately relaxed as she entered her favorite local haunt. It wasn't quite as lively as it could get yet, but it was getting there.

Unzipping her coat and letting it hang open, Evie traipsed through the bar and into the second room in back. This is where she knew her friends would be, and she gleefully glided toward their regular booth. Sitting on either side of that booth were Josh and Tamara, professors in the writing program, and a couple as well.

"Save some for me," teased Evie, arms out, interrupting Josh and Tamara's conversation. Evie was referring to the spicy potatoes that Josh was eating with a toothpick. The two looked up to Evie and celebrated.

"There she is!" said Tamara, who immediately scooted over to make way for her friend.

"Glad you could finally join us," said Josh.

"Sit, sit," said Tamara, patting the wooden bench.

"Don't mind if I do," said Evie. She removed her coat and hung it from a hook between booths, and then slid into the booth next to Tamara with her bag between them.

Tamara leaned over and kissed Evie on the cheek, and Evie did the same.

"Another semester begins," said Josh, lifting a pint glass of beer up toward Evie.

"So it does," agreed Evie. "Who's our waitress?" she said, looking around.

"Andrea," Tamara said. "She'll be back around soon."

"Good," said Evie, relaxing now into the booth and smiling. "I could use a drink."

"Oh, come on," said Josh. "It was only the first day back. How long was your class today, half an hour?"

"Josh, a half an hour is about my limit for work," said Evie dryly. "Anything beyond that, and I am absolutely *wiped*." Tamara and Josh laughed.

"Chronic fatigue?" said Tamara, lifting a brow.

"Existential ennui," corrected Evie, giving her friends another laugh.

"Well, hopefully you've got a good crop of students this semester," said Josh. "I got that guy you were talking about before in my lit class. The suck-up guy. David something or another."

"*Right!*" said Evie, nodding and pointing across the table at Josh. "I'm sorry to hear that. I dealt with him last semester."

"The guy won't shut up," said Josh in mock-seriousness. "It's the first class, and he's already talking about how he's read most of the novels *twice* but that he'll *certainly read them again* so they're fresh in his mind. I mean, guy, step back from the ledge." Evie and Tamara laughed.

"I was telling Josh he should take the guy aside," said Tamara. "And give him a different reading list. Something to test his mettle. Bury him in Pynchon for the semester or something."

"No," said Evie, picking a spicy potato from the plate in the center of the table and popping it into her mouth. Then she licked her fingers. "That'll backfire. A guy like that, he'll absolutely *revel* in the attention and he'll think he's teacher's pet. You'll never get rid of him, Josh. Soon he's got your cell phone number and he's showing up at your house unannounced."

"You could be right," said Josh. He sipped from his beer.

Just then, a pretty blonde girl approached the table. Her hair was pulled back, and she wore a white button-down shirt and a black apron around her waist. She smiled as she looked to Evie.

"Hi Evie," she said.

"Andrea, darling," said Evie. "So good of you to join us."

"I'm here all night," Andrea said, still smiling. "The usual?"

"Buffalo Trace, neat," Evie replied. "The usual."

"Got it," said Andrea. "Anything else?"

"Maybe another boat of spicy potatoes," said Evie. "And... guys?" she said, looking to her friends.

"Charcuterie?" asked Tamara.

"Charcuterie," replied Josh with a firm nod.

"And olives!" said Evie. "But can you do me a favor, Andrea?"

"Of course, Evie," said Andrea. "I know what you're going to ask."

"Extra pickled garlic," Evie said with excitement.

"Gross," said Tamara, shaking her head.

"Extra pickled garlic," confirmed Andrea, laughing. "I don't even know why I ask you guys what you want. You get the same thing every time."

"We don't need any lip," said Evie in a tease. "Just a lot of extra pickled garlic."

"Got it," said Andrea, smiling and rolling her eyes. She walked off from the table.

The three friends laughed and joked and caught up through the delivery of drinks and food. They always had a good time together. While they were all certainly friendly with the rest of the English and Writing department, the three of them hung around with each other the most. Really, though, Josh and Tamara hung around together because they were in a relationship. And Evie and Tamara went back as friends pretty far, well before teaching together at Westin. They got their own MFA degrees together in New York City.

"So," said Josh, taking a drink and then setting his glass down on the table. "Any noteworthy students in your workshop this semester?"

"Mmm," mused Evie, sipping from her glass of bourbon as she considered the question.

"You always get some doozies," Tamara said and grinned. "They all want to catch a glimpse of Evelyn Driscoll."

"Yeah, yeah," said Evie, waving Tamara off. "I think that trend is dying down. I haven't had a book out in seven years. That's an eternity. I bet half of these students have never even heard of me."

"You're very modest," teased Tamara. "I just want you to know that. We both think you're so very modest."

Evie rolled her eyes, smiled, took a drink.

"So... nobody?" asked Josh, returning to his original question. "No one sticks out?"

"There is this one young woman," said Evie carefully. "I don't know anything about her, really. Pretty, lively, spunky. There's definitely something about her. You can just look at her and tell there's something different in there."

"All right," said Josh. He looked to Tamara and shrugged.

"She came up to me after class," said Evie. "And she... well, she was kind of gushing over me. She asked if she could be in my thesis group next year."

"Next year?" said Tamara. "So she's a first year student already trying to pin down a thesis advisor?"

"Right," said Evie. "I mean, honestly, I can tell she's a fan. She said as much. But I don't know anything beyond that."

"What's her name?" asked Tamara.

"Meadow Sims," Evie said, taking another drink from her small glass.

"Ah," said Josh, eyes widening and nodding. "Yeah, I know her. She was in my workshop last semester. Red pen."

"Oh, so you know her," said Evie with slight excitement, gesturing at Josh. "What's her deal? Is she good? Is she weird? Is she *crazy*?"

"She's good," said Josh. "She's... really good. Evie, she's got a novel."

"I know," said Evie. "She told me that."

"We workshopped parts of it in class," said Josh. He took a deep breath and then exhaled. "I think you're going to like it. It very much does remind me of *The Hyacinth Hotel*."

"Huh," said Evie flatly. "Like, she's copping my style?"

"I wouldn't say that," corrected Josh. "I just mean... I think you're an obvious inspiration to her."

"Well, *shit*," sighed Evie, returning to her bourbon. She

swished some of the booze around in her mouth before she swallowed. "That really throws a wrench in things. I think she's cute. So if she's a good writer, too…"

"Oh, no no no!" Josh and Tamara said simultaneously, waving their hands back and forth.

"Evie, no," said Tamara. "Remember what happened to Wayne?"

"Of course I do," said Evie. "I'm well aware."

"The administration will not tolerate it," said Josh. "Getting involved with another professor, *fine*. Even an adjunct would be okay. But no current students."

"We teach grad school," countered Evie. "They're all adults. This one's somewhere in her mid-twenties."

"It's not about that," said Tamara. "You know it's a power dynamic thing. And you especially, someone of your stature, you can really make some of these students starstruck."

"I know," groaned Evie. "I know. You're right. Both of you. I need to keep this job. I definitely don't want to cross Dean Kelly. If I got canned, I'd be screwed. My advance for the next book is long spent. I've got to be good."

"If you're looking for love," said Tamara. "Hit the phone apps. Swipe this way, swipe that way."

"Yeah," said Evie, looking off somewhere else. She flattened her lips and nodded slowly. "Maybe I'll do that."

"Can you imagine matching with Evie on one of those dating apps?" said Josh, getting a good laugh out of it. He then mimed swiping the screen of a phone. "No, no, no…

wait. Didn't this lady win the American Novel Award?" Josh laughed again.

"I highly doubt most people on dating apps know about me or the American Novel Award," sniped Evie.

"Just be careful," said Tamara, seriousness in her voice. "We don't want to lose you."

"I know," said Evie, a smile returning to her face. She finished the rest of the bourbon in her glass and then looked to her friends. "I'll be good. Promise."

Josh and Tamara looked to one another. Their skepticism was obvious.

www.nicolettedane.com

AN EXCERPT: AN ACT OF LOVE

"I'm here with Liberty Logan," said the pretty aging brunette woman in a tight dress. Colleen Tate was her name, and she was one of the most well-known celebrity gossip peddlers on TV. "Liberty's hit comedy, *Conservatory*, is just about to enter its second season. Liberty, welcome to the show."

"Thank you," Liberty happily beamed. She had a girl-next-door look to her, with olive skin and dark hair. Liberty was fit and healthy, appearing to be younger than she actually was. "I'm happy to be here."

"Now, for our audience that hasn't yet seen your show," Colleen went on, implying the audience at home. They were shooting the interview in a studio in front of a few cameras and various crew members. "Can you give us a little summary of what it's about?"

"Sure," said Liberty. "It's an ensemble comedy, based around a conservatory. Plants, basically." She said, still smiling.

"Plants?" repeated Colleen.

"I know it sounds mundane," Liberty said. "But that's just the setting. It's about this group of people who work at the conservatory and the things they get into. It's a comedy of errors, really."

"I've seen the show and I think it's hilarious," said Colleen, grinning, leaning forward and placing her hand on Liberty's knee.

Liberty just looked down at the hand touching her for a moment, tried to ignore it, and then looked back up and put on a smile.

"Thank you," said Liberty. "That's sweet of you to say."

"It's a great cast," Colleen continued. "And people are really loving the interview, mockumentary style of it."

"It's fun to do," said Liberty. "We get to improvise some of the scenes, and the cast is really gelling. I think the audience is in for a treat with this new season."

"Now, on the show," Colleen said. "You're on-again, off-again with Kyle Hannigan's character, right?"

"Right," said Liberty. "I'm one of the botanists, and he's a janitor."

"But in real life," continued Colleen with a bit of trepidation. "You're a lesbian."

"That's true," said Liberty, offering a flat smile and a nod.

"Do you find there's any difficulty for you in portraying a straight woman on the show?" Colleen asked. Liberty couldn't help but make an incredulous face.

"No," said Liberty after a moment. "Kyle's character Shane is pretty feminine, so I guess it works out." Colleen chuckled, as the character of Shane was more of a buffoon than anything. Liberty could tell Colleen's amusement was fake.

"You're funny," said Colleen. She then looked to the camera. "She's funny."

"Thanks," mewed Liberty.

"We're going to go to a clip," said Colleen, holding a finger up. "Then we'll be right back with Liberty Logan."

Both Colleen and Liberty smiled and looked into the camera for what felt like a moment too long, and then the director stepped forward.

"Cut!" said the director. Almost immediately, two women ran up to where Colleen and Liberty sat and began to reapply makeup.

"Thanks for having me on," Liberty said softly.

"Oh, sure," Colleen replied nonchalantly. She didn't even look at Liberty. Instead, she took out her phone and looked down into the screen.

Liberty crossed her arms and straightened her lips, as her makeup artist blotted at her face. She was already eager to get out of there. Liberty hated these interviews, they always felt so phony. But there was nothing she could do. This was her life now.

When she stepped out of the sound stage, Liberty slipped her sunglasses down over her eyes and waltzed out into the studio lot. The interview with Colleen was on the same network as her show, and thus they filmed quite close. She wasn't on call to shoot today, but as she was already there, she decided to walk herself over to where *Conservatory* shot and see if she couldn't hang around with the cast.

After going through security with a smile and a wave, she wandered through the backstage area and down the row of dressing rooms. Liberty wasn't sure who might be around, and who might be shooting, but she figured she'd try her luck with Kyle. They had grown close since pairing up on screen, and she always enjoyed talking to him, especially when she was feeling down.

Liberty walked up to Kyle's dressing room door and she knocked. She waited. And then, after a moment, the door was yanked open unceremoniously and behind it stood Kyle. He was in boxers and a t-shirt and had a toothbrush in his mouth.

"Libby," Kyle said, removing the toothbrush. His mouth was splattered with foam. "To what do I owe the pleasure?"

"Go spit that out," said Liberty, pushing past Kyle and walking into his dressing room. "And put on some pants."

"No way," Kyle said, walking over to the bathroom to take Liberty's spitting advice. "If I put my pants on before my scene, they'll get wrinkled."

"You're a janitor!" protested Liberty, unable to suppress her laugh. "Your pants are already wrinkled."

"It's a mindset thing," Kyle replied, pointing to his head. He finished up brushing his teeth, wiped at his mouth, and joined Liberty in the dressing room. She was already sitting on the couch, while Kyle moved toward the chair in front of his makeup mirror and took a seat.

"I just came from doing an interview with *Tinsel Talk*," said Liberty, dropping her head back on the couch and putting her hand on her forehead. "Colleen Tate. Ugh. What a shit show that is."

"Yeah," agreed Kyle. "That Hollywood rag shit is tired. Makes you feel like you've always got to watch your back."

"I knew it was coming," said Liberty. "I mean, I intrinsically knew that this kind of stuff happened for famous actors, but I just never really thought about how it would affect me personally. It always felt so far off."

"Eh," said Kyle with an indifferent shrug. "It's a small price to pay for getting to do this for a living."

"Right," Liberty agreed, nodding slowly and trying to believe Kyle's words.

"You're not called today, are you?" Kyle said, furrowing his brow.

"No, I'm not shooting any scenes today," said Liberty. "That's why I did the interview. But I figured I'd stop by anyway."

"Cool," said Kyle.

"Otherwise, I would just go home," Liberty went on. "And, you know, rearrange my silverware or something."

"It's a beautiful day outside," said Kyle, pointing despite the fact that his dressing room had no windows. "The world's your oyster!"

"I know it is," said Liberty. "I know."

"So what's the problem, dude?" Kyle said, shrugging, arms wide.

"I don't know," said Liberty. "I guess, now that I've found this fame, even though I'm not like a mega star or anything, I just feel more lonely than ever."

"Ah," said Kyle, understanding immediately. "I get it. Libby, you want romance."

"I'd *love* some romance," said Liberty. "It's so weird. It's like, the more known you are, the more lonely you become. I only feel at home around you guys, around the show."

"I get it," said Kyle. "Totally, I get it."

"You're way more outgoing than me," said Liberty. "I'm such an introvert."

"Yeah, but I can still understand where you're coming from," said Kyle. "This new fame has been a little weird for me, too."

"How so?" asked Liberty dryly.

"I..." said Kyle, trailing off as he thought about it. "Well, now I have my own apartment and I'm not living on my buddy's couch anymore. Remembering to pay bills every month is *tough*."

"You're crazy," Liberty said, cracking a smile and shaking her head.

"Yeah," said Kyle, his tone changing to one of consolation. "I'm actually having a blast with my fame."

"And I'm sure you're pulling an entirely new level of chicks," Liberty said flippantly. "My pool of chicks to pull from at this level, well, it's pretty *dry*."

"I can see that," admitted Kyle.

"I'm sorry," Liberty said, sitting up straighter on the couch. "I didn't mean to dump all this on you. That interview just got me thinking about things and I needed someone to talk to."

"Oh, *dude*, anytime," said Kyle. "Don't feel you have to hold back from me. Despite our differences, we are in the same boat here. Some of the other people on the show, they already had a career before this. You and I, this is our big break."

"When I look to Kara," said Liberty, referring to Kara Stanton, the star of *Conservatory* and a comedy superstar. "I just think she handles this so well. She's so talented, and so friendly, and so together. I want to be like her."

"C'mon, Libby," said Kyle, waving a hand. "She's been doing this since the 90s. You can't compare yourself to her."

"I'm not really comparing, I guess," said Liberty. "I just want that feeling of having it together. And Kara, she so totally *exudes* that."

Suddenly, there was a knock at the door. Both Liberty and Kyle looked to the door as it opened up a crack. A head stuck in. It was one of the show's production assistants, a woman named Holly. Her hair was pulled tightly back in a ponytail and her black plastic glasses hung low on her nose.

"Kyle, we're ready for you," said Holly. "Hey, Liberty."

"Hey," replied Liberty gently.

"Now it's time for pants!" called out Kyle, standing up from his chair.

"Five minutes," said Holly. She then shut the door.

Liberty watched as Kyle hurriedly got dressed for his scene. She sighed and meditated on her life. She was so grateful for all of this. It was her dream come true. But she had yet to learn to navigate the intricacies of her newly acquired fame. It was tricky and confusing.

It made her think back to what life was like in the past. Liberty remembered where she came from, and she smiled easily.

Jessica Coleridge, a happy and positive blonde, walked out of the terminal at LAX wheeling a suitcase behind her. She looked around and marveled at how frantic everyone was. It gave her a small laugh, but then she immediately chastised herself for being so judgmental. She had no idea what they were going through. They could be late for wherever it was they had to go. They could be dealing with emergencies. Jessica stopped and put her hands together for a moment, practicing empathy for all the people around her that seemed so hectic.

It was Jessica's first time out in Los Angeles. In fact, she rarely left Colorado. She had grown up in Longmont and eventually settled in Boulder. She really felt no reason to leave apart from the various yoga retreats she went to, and her business of course. The insanity of big city life just wasn't for her. Boulder was her place to shine. However, a business opportunity had presented itself in Los Angeles and there she was. Standing outside of the airport trying to catch a cab.

Eventually a cab stopped near Jessica at the curb at arrivals, and the gruff looking cabbie quickly hopped out of his car, came around the front, and went for Jessica's suitcase. She smiled as he took it from her and rolled it back to the trunk.

"Should I just get in?" she asked. But the cabbie didn't respond. He probably didn't even hear her. Jessica stood there for a moment, still smiling, dressed comfortably in jelly flats, her form-fitted black yoga pants, and a light sweater made to look like herringbone out of some stretchy athletic material. After a moment, she shrugged to herself and got into the cab.

"Where to?" barked the cabbie, already putting the car into gear and speeding into the traffic of the airport avenue.

"Um," said Jessica, looking down into her phone and scrolling through an email. "Echo Park. I'm staying in a rental there as I open up a new yoga studio."

"Sure, sure," said the cabbie. "Echo Park." Reaching out, he turned up his radio just a little bit more.

Jessica smiled and nodded, trying to catch the cabbie's eyes in the rearview mirror but he never looked back at her. After another moment, Jessica gave up and looked out of the window, watching this new landscape move by her. It was a bright, sunny, warm day, even though it was technically autumn. While Colorado was already showing signs of the seasonal change, southern California still felt like summer. Jessica liked that.

Looking down to her phone, Jessica went over the email from the short-term rental agency again. Although she was certainly excited to be expanding her business, the prospect of coming out to LA alone, and without her business partner Quinn, left her feeling a bit lost and stranded. She knew she would be keeping busy, but Jessica was a social woman, she liked the companionship of others, but she had arrived in Los Angeles without knowing another soul anywhere around.

But then it hit her. Flipping over to her contacts, Jessica quickly scrolled through them until she laid her eyes on the name of an old friend. She and Liberty had grown up together, they had been very close for a while, but had lost touch over the recent years. Jessica remembered that Liberty had left Colorado to try to be an actress in LA, and while she had no idea what her old friend could be up to now, she figured that it was worth a shot to reach out and rekindle an old friendship.

Without any further deliberation, which wasn't Jessica's style, she hit the call button and put her phone to her ear. She smiled as she listened to the ring.

After a handful of rings, the call was answered.

"Hello?" Liberty said with slight confusion on the other line. "Jessica Coleridge?"

"Liberty Logan!" Jessica replied. "How are you?"

"Oh, not bad," said Liberty. She was putting up her defenses and treading carefully. Since she had become a known celebrity, she had learned to take care of her privacy just a little bit more. "How are you?"

"I'm really good," said Jessica. "I know it's weird for me to be calling, seeing as we haven't talked in so long. But a business thing has brought me to Los Angeles and I'm probably going to be here through the new year. I remembered that you moved to Los Angeles years ago to be an actress, and I'm just taking a shot that you're still here."

"I'm still here," replied Liberty. She was confused, but intrigued by Jessica's words. "Yeah, still acting. You're here on business?"

"Right," Jessica said, positivity apparent in her voice. "I run a chain of yoga studios and we're opening one here. It's a whole *thing*, but whatever to that. We should meet up! I know the acting thing can be hard, but I'm doing super well and I'm happy to treat. I'd really just like to see my old friend."

Liberty was floored. It struck her pretty plainly that Jessica had no idea that she was on a hit show. It gave Liberty a laugh, it was so absurd. How could she not know?

"Wow," Liberty replied after a moment. "Yeah. It would be great to see you, Jess. And don't worry about all that... I'm doing fine, too."

"Yeah?" said Jessica. "That's great to hear! I mean, great that you're doing well *and* that you'll hang out. If I'm being totally honest, you're the only person I know out here and I just didn't want to spend my time in LA all alone." Jessica laughed at herself and her candor.

"Oh, c'mon," countered Liberty. "The Jessica I always knew never had problems making friends."

"Okay, *guilty*," said Jessica. "You're right. I'm sure I'll meet some fun and exciting people in time. But why not catch up with a friend from the past?"

"Why not," repeated Liberty with a smile. "So where are you staying?"

"I'm in Echo Park," affirmed Jessica. "I got a rental there for six months, it's all furnished and everything. That's where I'm opening up the new studio. Echo Park."

"That's a hip neighborhood," said Liberty. "I bet you'll do well there."

"I sure hope so!" said Jessica. "We're putting a lot of money into this and... No. No more business talk right now. Let's get together, catch up, and I'll tell you all about it then."

"Great," said Liberty. "Why don't you get settled and we'll meet up tomorrow night?"

"Tomorrow night it is," Jessica replied happily. "It's so great to reconnect with you Liberty and I'm really looking forward to seeing you now. It's been far too long. Probably almost ten years."

"I'd say about ten years, yeah."

"Too long," repeated Jessica. "Okay, I'll let you get back to whatever it is you were doing. Feel free to text or call and let me know what tomorrow looks like for you. I'll be getting settled and doing a little work in the morning, but don't feel like you're interrupting if you want to reach out."

"That's great," said Liberty. She felt refreshed in talking

to Jessica. She felt as though Jessica was from a completely different world. Her old world, a world she found herself missing. Her heart filled with happiness. "I'll talk to you then."

"Take care, Liberty," said Jessica with a smile. "Have a wonderful day!"

"You too," said Liberty. "Bye Jess."

Liberty hung up her phone and set it on top of her counter in front of her. She sat back in her chair in front of the mirror, lights shining bright at her, while one of her usual makeup artists, a young woman named Ream, returned to work after pausing for Liberty's phone call.

"That was a really old friend of mine," mused Liberty as Ream dabbed at her face with a small sponge.

"Is she like in her 90s or something?" Ream replied in a bored tone.

"Even older," said Liberty, playing along. "She's over 100."

"That's definitely an old friend."

"No, you jerk," said Liberty teasingly. "A friend from growing up. From Colorado."

"That's cool," said Ream.

"The weird thing is," Liberty continued. "I don't think she knows that I'm on this show... or anything like that."

"She doesn't know you're an actress?" Ream tried to clarify, bent at her waist and getting in close to Liberty's face as she worked.

"Well, she knows I'm an actress," said Liberty. "But I don't think she knows the extent of it."

"Oh," Ream said with little emotion.

"Super weird," mused Liberty, slouching back. "Really weird to be hearing from her."

"Yeah."

"Do you watch the show?" Liberty asked with a hint of self-consciousness.

"Sure," said Ream. "I like it. It's pretty funny."

"Okay," said Liberty, staring off into the mirror, looking into her own eyes as she mulled it all over.

Jessica's call was certainly intriguing. And Liberty found herself looking forward to meeting with her more than she'd looked forward to anything in a long while.

www.nicolettedane.com